RANDOM HOUSE
CHILDREN'S BOOKS
A DIVISION OF RANDOM HOUSE, INC.

TITLE: The True Adventures of Nicolò Zen
AUTHOR: Nicholas Christopher
IMPRINT: Alfred A. Knopf Books for Young Readers
PUBLICATION DATE: January 7, 2014
ISBN: 978-0-375-86738-5
Price: $17.99 U.S./$19.99 CAN.
GLB ISBN: 978-0-375-96738-2
GLB Price: $20.99 U.S./$24.00 CAN.
EBOOK ISBN: 978-0-375-89786-3
Pages: 304
Ages:12 & up

Please send any review or mention
of this book to:
Random House Children's Books Publicity Department
1745 Broadway, Mail Drop 9-1
New York, NY 10019

rhkidspublicity@randomhouse.com

THE TRUE ADVENTURES OF NICOLO ZEN

a novel

Nicholas Christopher

ALFRED A. KNOPF
New York

THIS IS A BORZOI BOOK PUBLISHED BY ALFRED A. KNOPF

Visit us on the Web! randomhouse.com/teens

Educators and librarians, for a variety of teaching tools,
visit us at RHTeachersLibrarians.com

Library of Congress Cataloging-in-Publication Data
Christopher, Nicholas.
The true adventures of Nicolo Zen : a novel / Nicholas Christopher. — First edition.
p.   cm.
Summary: "Orphan Nicolo Zen is all alone in 1700s Venice, save for his clarinet, enchanted by a mysterious magician to allow its first player to perform expertly. Soon Nicolo is a famous virtuoso, wealthy beyond his dreams, but he can't stop wondering if he earned the success—or if the girl he met in Venice is safe from the harm." —Provided by publisher
ISBN 978-0-375-86738-5 (trade) — ISBN 978-0-375-96738-2 (lib. bdg.) —
ISBN 978-0-375-89786-3 (ebook) — ISBN 978-0-375-86492-6 (pbk.)
[1. Musicians—Fiction. 2. Clarinet—Fiction. 3. Magic—Fiction. 4. Love—Fiction. 5. Italy—History—1559–1789—Fiction.] I. Title.
PZ7.N5113Tr 2014
[Fic]—dc23
2013012853

The text of this book is set in 11-point Goudy Oldstyle.

Printed in the United States of America

January 2014

10 9 8 7 6 5 4 3 2 1

First Edition

For Constance, in Venice

CONTENTS

I
The Orphanage

1

When the Master auditioned us, we were told not to speak.

Luca, his assistant, a heavyset man in a black coat, handed each of us a page of sheet music, from the first movement of the Master's latest concerto. "Just play this," he said gruffly, pulling at his black beard, "first in D major, then in B-flat minor."

Two girls stood alongside me, one a violinist, the other a flautist. We were at the center of a long, poorly lit room in the rear of the church. It smelled of beeswax and lemon oil. The worn oak planks creaked beneath our feet. On one wall, there was a large portrait of our Doge, Giovanni Cornaro, who never smiled, facing a small portrait of Pope Clement. Even at the age of fourteen, I knew that in any city besides Venice, in the year 1714, the Pope's portrait would have been the larger one. The Master was sitting in a high-backed chair against the wall, about twenty feet away. It felt like a mile, and I would learn that, even in close quarters, the Master seemed distant and remote. His head was bowed. His red hair flowed over his shoulders. He wore a yellow jacket, black pants, and boots with silver buckles. He never looked at us.

The violinist played first, but was so nervous she barely reached the middle of the piece before lowering her instrument and fighting back tears. The flautist played fearlessly, but made several errors, and out of the corner of my eye I saw Luca shaking his head.

When she was done, he nodded to me, and I stepped up to the music stand. My clarinet was constructed of ivory, its keys and spring gold, and even in that dim light the instrument shone when I raised it to my lips. I played the piece, an intricate saraband, in both keys as energetically as I could.

When I finished, the Master raised his head for the first time and peered at me. I felt his blue eyes were searching out my innermost self, and I prayed he would not find it.

"A clarinet," he said. "I have only heard the instrument played twice before. Never in Venice. Never so well. Come here and show it to me."

I tried to conceal my nervousness as I approached his desk. He examined the clarinet closely and handed it back to me. "A beautiful instrument. The ones I saw were ebony. This is unusual. Do you always play the part of the score written for flute?"

I nodded.

"Perhaps one day the clarinet will have its own part. Go back to your seat." He looked at Luca. "She will do," he said.

I sighed with relief, but not, as you might think, because he approved of my playing or was intrigued by my clarinet, but because Master Antonio Vivaldi had just admitted me, a boy named Nicolò Zen, to his orchestra, all of whose members were girls from the Ospedale della Pietà, the orphanage for girls attached to the Church of La Pietà.

When Luca asked for my full name and my father's name, I replied, "Nicolà. Nicolà Vitale. Daughter of Giacomo Vitale."

One lie after another, which he wrote down in the brown book he carried with him at all times.

 4

2

How had I disguised myself?

With great difficulty.

I was slim-waisted, with large eyes and long brown hair. People thought me good-looking, but I had never been mistaken for a girl, and without altering my appearance, I never would be. I was fortunate to know something about girls, the way they dressed and moved and combed their hair, from having grown up with three sisters.

I was raised on the small, wooded island of Mazzorbo in the Lagoon, where my father eked out a living as a handyman and part-time tar mixer at the boatyard. He was also a fine fisherman—his own father's profession—and one of my fondest memories of him is our rowing out to the deeper waters off the island of Burano, just the two of us, to catch a basketful of striped bass, the tastiest fish in the Lagoon, which my mother would fry for dinner. Usually we brought home enough to feed the entire family for several days.

My parents and my sisters contracted malaria when it wiped out most of our village. As with the nearby, and more famous, island of Torcello, Mazzorbo's misty swamps were infested with mosquitoes. When they hatched in the spring rain, the mosquitoes carried the disease among us quickly, and dozens of people perished each day. I ran a fever so high that my eyes burned and my tongue stuck to the roof of my mouth, until eventually, dizzy and short of breath, I blacked out. It was a miracle I survived. Thus, in addition to my ability to play the clarinet, and despite my true gender, I met a crucial qualification for the orchestra: I was an orphan. Sadly, that was no lie.

When my fever broke, I awoke from a restless sleep and at first had no memory of what had occurred. I was lying on a straw bed in an unfamiliar house. There was a crucifix hanging from the bedpost and an icon of the Savior nailed to the wall across from me. An elderly widow, a stout woman with curly white hair, was swabbing my forehead with a wet cloth. I had seen her around the village carrying baskets of laundry, for that was her business, serving the island's rich landowners. Her name was Signora Capelli. Someone had carried me to her house when I was found wandering the streets two nights earlier. It was she who told me what I already knew but still could not believe: my entire family was gone. In quick succession, delirious with fever, they had succumbed to the disease. I was completely on my own. Signora Capelli had no idea where my family was buried.

"They were burying people a dozen at a time in unmarked graves," she said. "God help us."

Signora Capelli had kindly washed my clothes, and before I left her house she fed me a breakfast of cornmeal and honey. I thanked her, and promised myself that one day I would repay her kindness.

It was a hot, damp day, a foul wind blowing from the swamps. I walked down several lanes, to the other side of the village, the landmarks of my childhood—Signor Raguso's bakery, the produce market, the glazier's workshop—replaced by one scene of horror after another. Men and women wailing in grief, tearing at their hair; children in their death throes, their eyes rolled back in their heads; and corpses everywhere, giving off a stench that made me gag. There were corpses piled in carts, like Signor Raguso and his wife, laid on ragged stretchers; like Carla, the butcher's daughter, sprawled out in the baking mud, as I would have been had some Good Samaritan not carried me to the widow's house. I prayed I would never see such things again.

I reached my own home, and at the sight of it burst into tears. The house was empty. My family had indeed been buried already, and neither our one surviving neighbor, Signor Tramante, nor a grim, exhausted constable could tell me where. For an instant, I had a wild glimmer of hope that perhaps one of my sisters had also wandered off feverish, like me, and was being nursed back to health. But, no, Signor Tramante was certain he had seen the stretcher carriers take five bodies out of the house.

I had awoken to a nightmare that could not be escaped. I packed a few articles of clothing in the canvas bag my mother used to take to the market. Then I put in my father's knife, in its leather sheath, and my clarinet, which I kept hidden under my bed. Sitting at our kitchen table for the last time, numb with grief, I suddenly felt as if I had stepped out of my own body, which was why I didn't hear someone open the door behind me and enter the house.

It was our landlord, Signor Cardinale, a thin, hatchet-faced man with cold eyes who was suspicious of everything and everyone. Unlike any other man I encountered that day, he was shaved and neatly dressed, wearing a blue cloak and polished boots—as if nothing had changed and all was well with the world.

With no word of condolence, no gesture of solace—not even a greeting—he informed me in his high, squeaky voice that he was reclaiming our poor cottage.

"Your father was two months behind in the rent, so this was going to happen one way or the other. I am boarding up the house, and no one will be permitted inside until I rent it again. Take your things and go on your way."

My mother, who had seldom spoken ill of anyone, detested this man, but until that moment I hadn't known just how wicked and depraved he was.

I added her bronze bracelet to my bag, and my sister Alessandra's wooden comb, but it was too painful for me to sift through the rest of my family's meager possessions, especially with Signor Cardinale watching over me—as if I were a thief and this was not my own home.

Following me outside, he reached into his pocket and offered me a single zecchetto. I looked into his crimped face and fixed it in my memory, a reminder that I should always beware of men whose greed feeds, not just on treasure, but cruelty. Then, without a word, I turned on my heel and walked away.

"You won't get far in life with that attitude," he called after me, pocketing his zecchetto.

In fact, I got as far as I needed to that day, riding the packet boat across the Lagoon to Venice. And I will not pretend I mourned when I learned sometime later that, after repossessing countless other houses from destitute survivors of the epidemic, Signor Cardinale had contracted malaria himself and died horribly, choking on his own blood. As the boat pulled away from the dock, I sat alone in the stern, clutching my bag, and gazed back over Mazzorbo one last time. It looked no different than before—mist rising in the forest, wild ducks navigating the reeds, light shimmering on the water—but its natural beauty was like some cruel joke to me, knowing as I did how much suffering and death had descended on the island.

It was sunset when the steeples and towers of Venice came into view, glittering gold. We sailed past the forbidding sea-wall that encircled the Franciscan monastery on San Michele, where the monks buried their dead one on top of the other in the crowded cemetery. I shuddered to think of my parents and sisters in a shallow grave, cold as the earth itself now. It was unbearable. But I was alive, and I imagined my mother saying that there must be a reason for this, and that I must make the most of it and live my life, not just for myself, but for them.

This was small comfort for a boy entering a city alone at nightfall, poorly dressed, hungry, with no money and no place to stay, and only two immediate choices before him: to become a thief or a beggar. Which, for me, was no choice at all.

3

Thus it was that, the moment I set foot in Venice, I began to beg. From the docks of the Canareggio I followed a succession of dizzying alleys to the Grand Canal. I often lost my way in the darkness, zigzagging and backtracking, sometimes passing the same doorway two or three times. The air was pungent with smoke and the smell of cooking, which made me linger whenever I passed a tavern.

Though my family had lived just three hours away, we used to visit the city together but twice a year: in March, to be blessed on the Feast Day of San Stefano, and in September to watch the regatta, which the Doge himself initiated. Perched on a high platform in his gold chair, his robe adorned with every type of fish in the sea, he would drop his sea-blue scarf into the crowd below and toss a medallion, minted with his own image, into the canal.

My father traveled to Venice more frequently, and as I grew older, brought me along. We usually went first to a bacaro on the Calle Bartolomeo where he drank raboso wine from the barrel with a group of masons who were once his coworkers. Then I accompanied him to the boatyard on the Rio di San Trovaso where he bought a keg of tar that was sent to him in Mazzorbo. Once he took me to the Church of Santi Apostoli on the Strada Nuova, where he'd had his fateful accident one frigid morning, falling from a scaffold. In the coming days, I would revisit that church many times, sitting in the courtyard and gazing up at the steeple, one of the tallest in the city, knowing some of its limestone blocks had been hewn and mortared by my father's hands when he still had two good arms.

But that night, as the wind grew colder and the darkness deepened, on my own for the first time in my life, I found the city far stranger and more forbidding. My warm memories of my family and our former home already felt like part of another life, which I could never reenter. Though I had few possessions, in my grief and sadness I felt as if I were carrying a tremendous weight. If we're all allotted a certain amount of happiness in this life, I was certain that, despite my youth, I had used up all of mine and had only to look forward to a maze of fearful shadows and dead ends, resembling the maze of alleys I was trying to negotiate.

Finally I saw the lights of the Doge's Palace and the Campanile, whose bells were just striking ten o'clock. Skirting San Marco, where watchmen were making their rounds with swinging lanterns, and the Palace Guard in black capes marched around the perimeter, I made my way along the Riva degli Schiavoni and stopped just beyond the Rio dei Greci, where I began to beg. The dark waters of the Grand Canal glittered and the rooms of the great palazzi glowed with candlelight. The silhouettes of gentlemen in tall hats and ladies with mountainous hair glided back and forth. Streams of people swarmed past me, gaily dressed, talking and laughing. Scents of expensive powder and cologne filled my nostrils. Crowds gathered at the piers from which traghetti carried them across the canal to the Dorsoduro. Through the mist the windows of the Customs House were lit up, even at that hour, and on the roof, atop a golden ball, the bronze figure of *Fortune* served as a weather vane, moving this way and that in the wind.

Once I had caught my breath, I attempted to emulate the gestures and demeanor of the professional beggars I had seen on Burano on market days, when the lacemakers and potters peddled their wares. But I soon realized I could collect far more coins by playing my clarinet with my cap at my feet than by holding out an empty hand and wearing a doleful expression. I also needed to take myself to a quieter—though not too quiet—thoroughfare where I would not be lost in the throng. So I made my way along the canal to San Samuele and began to play my clarinet. Within a half hour, my hat was filled with enough soldi and denari—and a single zecchetto—to buy a meal, and even a proper coat the following day. But not enough to pay for a place to sleep, so for two nights, after playing for nearly sixteen straight hours, I curled up on a bench in the Campo San Vio, my head tucked into my coat and a bowl of hot soup in my stomach. Both nights, an old man was lying on another bench with his back to me, a tattered blanket barely covering him. The soles of his boots hung loose and his hands were nearly blue, like a dead man's. The second night, I found him in exactly the same position, and I feared he might have died. I watched him for a long while, hoping he would stir, and when he did finally, shifting one of his feet, I felt relieved, though I knew he surely had little time remaining on this earth.

By my third day in Venice, I had accumulated enough money to pay for a bed in a room with two others in a ramshackle boardinghouse on the Calle Bontini, near the boatyard. The smell of boiling tar reminded me of my father, and my first night there I wept. But I kept my guard up, too, for I was sharing the room with two grown men, shabbily dressed, and I knew enough to be wary when the fat one, named Filippo, blew out the candles as we

 12

got into our beds. Especially after the scrawny one, Giorgio, with ferret teeth and blotched cheeks, told me I had "pretty hair, like a girl."

This kept me from a good night's sleep, but it also planted the seed—which might never have blown into my head on its own— that would come to fruition two days later when Luca stopped to hear me play before a knot of people by the Palazzo Dandolo. I had replaced my wool cap with a floppy black hat, from which my hair flowed, and a long coat that concealed my figure. Luca listened until I finished the piece—a Scarlatti sonata—then nodded approvingly.

When I stooped to pick the coins from my bag, he asked me my age.

"Fourteen," I replied softly, and because my voice was naturally high, and yet to acquire timbre, I could make it very soft indeed.

"And what is that you're playing—a chalumeau?"

"No, sir, a clarinet."

"Where do you live?"

"I lived on Mazzorbo, sir, until a few days ago, when the epidemic carried off my family and the landlord took away our house."

"Your parents are dead?"

I nodded. "And my sisters. I was the youngest girl," I added.

"And you have no home?"

"No, sir. I have only my clarinet and these pennies you see in my bag."

He scrutinized me closely. "And your name?"

"Nicolà," I replied after a moment's hesitation.

That moment was to alter the course of my entire life.

You see, I had recognized Luca. The previous evening, I had gone to the Ospedale della Pietà to hear the orchestra of orphan girls play. The usher had allowed me to stand in the back. The girl musicians performed in a gallery above the altar, partially concealed from the audience behind an iron grille. The Master conducted them with a fierce energy. And Luca sat in a box above, surveying them with a critical eye. I knew that a good number of these girls, when they came of age, were recruited into professional orchestras, not only in Venice, but Padua, Ravenna, and other cities. There were good musical ensembles in some of the city's other ospedali—especially the Mendicanti and the Incurabiliti, on the Zattere—but none compared to the Pietà's. As I listened to the girls, I thought how wonderful it must be to be one of them, and to play such music. And all at once I hatched a scheme. I saw an opportunity, not only to fulfill my father's grand prophesy that one day I would become a famous musician, but also to attend to the far more mundane and urgent need to get myself off the street, out of danger, with a secure roof over my head. It was a wild, desperate chance that would require plenty of luck, but I had nothing to lose.

So it was no accident that the next morning, disguising my gender as best I could, I chose a spot not fifty yards from the Ospedale della Pietà to play my clarinet, hoping Luca or the Master or someone who worked for them would hear me. How lucky I was, indeed, that it turned out to be Luca himself.

I was an orphan, but there was no orphanage for boys comparable to the Ospedale della Pietà, and certainly none with its own orchestra. The local orphanages for boys were in a woeful state, some just a step up from dungeons. The best of them was a warren of overcrowded rooms in a run-down annex of the Dominican seminary, whose monks were reputed to take pleasure in punishing the inmates. The wards who survived these grim establishments were sent into the world when they turned sixteen to do thankless work as oarsmen on commercial galleys or night laborers in the bowels of the Arsenal, assisting the shipbuilders. Only a fortunate few were apprenticed to prosperous tradesmen. With due respect to his memory, I did not want to follow my father's path in life, doing backbreaking work at the mercy of overseers and living in constant fear of poverty.

Now I had my chance at something better—even if I had to begin as an impostor. Having grown up with three beloved sisters—Carla, Rhea, and Alessandra—I knew a few things about how girls dressed, carried themselves, and spoke. I had even learned some of their more private habits, living as we did in three small rooms with a wooden bathtub and an outdoor privy. My sisters and I shared the same bedroom, which had two beds. Until the age of eight, I slept beside Carla, the youngest, who was ten, and dressed with all of them; only when Rhea was twelve and Alessandra thirteen did my mother sling a hammock for me near the fireplace in the kitchen, where I was also expected to dress.

Luca told me the Master was about to conduct auditions, open to "outsiders," who of course must be orphans, for two places in the orchestra that had been vacated unexpectedly.

"Can you read music?"

"Yes, sir. I learned in the church choir."

"Good. Those who are chosen in the auditions will become residents of the Ospedale as well as members of the orchestra. Consider this an invitation to attend."

"Thank you, sir."

"Get yourself a clean dress, Nicolà," he said, dropping two soldi into my bag and glancing disapprovingly at my rough shirt and pantaloons. "And be on time. Friday, at noon."

16

4

I did not like the idea of dressing up as a girl—really dressing up, not just hiding behind a greatcoat—but I swallowed my pride and stuck to my plan. When I wavered, I had only to remind myself of the alternatives: playing on the street for coins and sharing a room with the likes of Filippo and Giorgio, or entering a boys' orphanage.

I bought my dress that afternoon at a cluttered shop off the Campo San Polo. It cost me everything I had in my pocket, including Luca's contribution, so I had no supper that night, and the following day ate only some discarded produce—an overripe apple, a turnip, and some carrot greens—that I found at the market by the Rialto Bridge. I told myself it didn't matter that, waiting for Friday to come, I was too nervous to eat, anyway—and maybe I was. At the same time, I didn't want to faint from hunger at the audition.

I was looking for a dress that was not just adequate, but eye-catching, as my sisters would have advised. The one I picked out with Signora Gramani, the dressmaker, was green linen trimmed with lace. With her trained eye, Signora Gramani was suspicious of me, but asked no questions.

She clearly thought something was amiss when I insisted on using the curtained-off changing room reserved for her well-to-do clients.

"Come, child, you can try it on right here," she said. "It's quite private, and men seldom enter my shop."

But I insisted on going into the changing room, and when I emerged and she wouldn't look me in the eye, I knew I had confirmed her suspicions. Venice was a city of exotic tastes and loose morals, so I would certainly not have been the strangest customer she ever served. But I believe the reason she treated me kindly was simply that she was kindhearted. She chose the proper stockings to go with my dress, and a blue shawl, and persuaded the shopkeeper next door to sell me a pair of green brocaded slippers at half price.

Margarita Gramani was a handsome, dark-eyed woman, widowed when her husband, a Navy captain, was killed in a sea battle with the Genoans. At forty, I thought, she was too young to be a widow. She sent me on my way with a kiss on the cheek, and as with Signora Capelli, I swore that someday, somehow, I would repay her kindness—a bold vow for someone who couldn't even buy a crust of bread.

5

On Friday morning at my boardinghouse, I waited for Giorgio and Filippo to leave—both of them badly hungover from the previous night—then prepared myself with care before a broken piece of mirror I had salvaged. I washed and combed my hair, and courtesy of Signora Gramani, brushed a touch of rouge onto my cheeks—the faintest blush—and extended my eyelashes with a small lead stick. After putting on my new outfit, I went out the back door, so as to avoid the residents who might recognize me.

Walking along the canal to La Pietà in my dress, I had my first lesson in the indignities suffered by girls. Of course, I had seen the way men looked at my sisters, especially Alessandra, who was very beautiful, with full breasts and hips. And I had overheard some of the rough men my father worked with talk about women. But it is different when you yourself are the target of oglers, and men who offer up crude remarks, and worst of all, men like the fat baker I encountered in an alley who was free with his hands, pinching my bottom and grabbing my dress where my breasts would have been if I had breasts. I kicked him in the shin and ran. And I realized that if I was going to pull off this masquerade, such abuse was the price I would have to pay, and it wasn't going to get any easier.

At the church a blind boy named Aldo led me to the room where I would audition. He must have been around sixteen, broad-shouldered, with a long face and large ears. His sad, sly eyes seemed to be coated with a thin white film, like milk. His hands were oversized for his body and hung so heavily that they seemed to weigh down his arms and shoulders so that his fingertips reached well below his knees. He wore a sheepskin vest that smelled of sheep and a blue skullcap of rough wool that barely concealed his black curls. I thought it odd that a blind boy should be my guide, but would discover that Aldo knew his way around every nook and cranny of the church, from the basement to the steeple, and never missed a step or bumped into things. It was as if he had antennae, like an insect, and a detailed map of the Ospedale in his head. He came and went in the vestry, the rehearsal rooms, the Master's quarters, and even the dormitory, where, after all, there was no chance of his seeing the girls undressed or otherwise. In fact, the girls were led to believe that his presence was no more threatening than that of a eunuch in a Turkish harem.

Like many blind people, Aldo's lack of vision had sharpened his other senses: he could hear and smell things the rest of us couldn't. Perhaps that was why he sniffed the air around me in the audition room with a puzzled expression. He is more suspicious of me than Signora Gramani, I thought, taking a seat beside the violinist and the flautist, as far from Aldo as I could get. Can he actually smell that I'm a boy, not a girl? I asked myself.

I would soon find out.

6

Shortly after I passed the audition, Luca informed me that the Master would now interview me in his office. In my ignorance, I hadn't expected this, and I grew anxious trying to imagine the questions he would ask. More importantly, I realized that speaking softly would no longer be enough: from now on, beginning with the Master, I would have to disguise my voice during every conversation. I knew the best course was to answer his questions truthfully, adhering to my actual history, except for the matter of my gender. That way there was only one lie I could be caught out in. It was a big lie, and I wasn't much of a liar, with no experience of lying on a scale like this, but I told myself that if I stuck to a simple set of answers, no matter how complicated the questions, I would be all right.

This shaky logic left me uneasy as Luca escorted me down a corridor and ushered me through a tall yellow door. In the Master's office the heels of my new shoes clicked sharply on the brick floor. It was a sunny day, but heavy drapes were drawn over the windows and a pair of burning candles flanked a cluttered desk. Bent over a piece of sheet music, humming to himself, the Master was writing with a black quill.

He nodded toward a chair wedged between two piles of books and musical scores. "Sit, Nicolà, and tell me how you came by your clarinet and where you learned to play it."

Again I was caught off guard. Preoccupied with my masquerade, fearful of exposure, expecting trick questions, I was not prepared for such an obvious one. Nor for the shock of finding myself alone with Venice's greatest musician, and hearing him utter my assumed name. Trying to grasp the fact that I was there because *he* was interested in *me*. After suffering through the worst week of my life, I couldn't believe my good fortune.

"Well?" the Master said.

"I come from Mazzorbo," I began. "My father was a mason. A good one. One day he fell from a scaffold while working at the Church of Santi Apostoli. He was lucky he wasn't killed. But he broke his arm and it never healed properly. So then he mixed tar at the boatyard and did small jobs to support all of us. Last year he was hired to build a fireplace for a glovemaker, Signor Benito Agnetti, who lived in the Giudecca. When Father completed the work, Signor Agnetti confessed that he didn't have the money to pay him. Father threatened to complain to the local constable, and if necessary, to the Giudecca's commissioner, who is one of the Doge's councillors. Signor Agnetti grew fearful and, without thinking, told my father that, in lieu of ducats, he could take any object in his shop as payment. He soon regretted that he hadn't been more specific, for expecting my father to pick out the most expensive pair of gloves, Signor Agnetti was stunned to see my father—who wore only masonry gloves—eyeing objects with which Agnetti had dressed up the shop: a crystal pitcher, a Moroccan dagger with a silver handle, and most valuable of all, an oval mirror from Murano. But Signor Agnetti breathed a sigh of relief when my father chose this clarinet, which caught his eye suddenly on a high shelf."

"You must know it is a relatively new instrument," the Master said.

I shook my head.

"You don't. Do you know anything about its origins?"

"No, sir."

"You know only how to play it," he said skeptically. "All right. I'll give you a short history. Twenty years ago, in Nuremberg, Germany, a man named Denner took the chalumeau, which was like a shepherd's pipe, with a single reed and nine holes, and improved upon it. He gave it a proper embouchure and added two holes above the duodecime key, enabling the clarinet to produce both upper and lower registers, pitched somewhere between an oboe and a trumpet, but with greater range than either. I wondered when I would encounter another clarinetist, but I never dreamed it would be a girl your age. Your instrument is more beautifully crafted than the one I saw in Milan. It must be worth a great deal."

More than my father ever imagined, I wanted to say. "Signor Agnetti told my father the clarinet was a gift from his cousin, who lived in San Polo and had no use for it. Signor Agnetti gave my father the impression that he and his cousin were not on the best of terms. Knowing I loved music, and learned to read scores while singing at our church, my father chose the clarinet for me, though he didn't know what it was. He encouraged me to play it. We were a poor family, and he could easily have sold it instead."

"He was a good man," the Master nodded approvingly, and I could see he had enjoyed the story. "So that is how you acquired the clarinet. And now I've given you its history. But I asked you where you learned to play it—in just one year, apparently," he added, with a raised eyebrow. "Who was your teacher?"

I became tongue-tied, trying to invent a name.

"Who taught you?" he prodded me.

I decided to tell the truth. "I had no teacher."

He sat back in his chair. "You would have me believe you are self-taught, and on such a unique instrument?"

I nodded.

His eyes narrowed. "All right. I would like to hear more about that."

My mind was racing, but I spoke carefully. "As I said, I learned music from Father Michele at the Church of Santa Caterina on Mazzorbo."

"I know Father Michele," the Master said.

"You do?" I said, barely getting the words out.

"We were ordained the same year. I am acquainted with most of the priests in the archdiocese."

I knew the Master was a priest—"the Red Priest," people called him, on account of his hair—but even there in his own church he didn't look or sound like one to me, not like Father Michele or any other priest.

"I don't see Father Michele often," he went on, "but at Christmas we dine at the Bishop's residence with our brethren."

I began to panic. My mouth went dry. And it took all my energy to appear calm. Christmas was nine months off, but if the Master should mention to Father Michele that a girl named Nicolà Vitale, who sang in his choir, had recently joined the orchestra at the Ospedale, and Father Michele replied, as he must, that he had never heard of such a girl, the game would be up. At best, I would appear to be a conniving and deceitful girl; at worst,

 24

I would be exposed as a brash impostor. Either way, it would result in my expulsion from the Ospedale.

"After choir practice at my church," I continued, "I attempted to play the hymns we sang on my clarinet. When troubadours visited Mazzorbo, I played along with them from a distance—where they couldn't hear me. I also went into the woods each day and echoed the birdsongs, note for note."

"Birdsongs?"

"Yes, the sparrows and starlings and the wild canaries, with their high pitch."

The Master smiled. "And in what key do the sparrows sing, Nicolà?"

"G major, usually."

He tucked his thumbs into his vest pockets and studied me more closely. "So you're another Orpheus, eh? Do you know who Orpheus was?"

I shook my head.

"No? Well, tell me about your family. Luca said they died in the epidemic. I am sorry to hear it. You had brothers and sisters?"

"Three sisters. And a brother, Alessandro," I added hastily, thinking I had better make sure to establish that there was a boy in the Zen family of Mazzorbo, in case inquiries were made. Except that the inquiries—and who exactly did I imagine would be making them?—would be about the *Vitale* family, Nicolà's family, which did not exist; the only Zen on Mazzorbo with a name like Nicolà was one Nicolò Zen, who had disappeared. It was all very confusing. After having convinced myself there was only one lie I could be caught out in, I quickly discovered that one lie leads to another, and another, and another, until finally it's not just the truth, but your own lies that you can't keep straight.

"You must miss your family," the Master said.

"I do," I replied, trying not to fidget with my dress, but relieved that at last I was speaking honestly.

"You have a home here now. You will live in good clean quarters, be provided with clothing and necessities, eat hot meals, and otherwise be protected from the hardships and dangers of the world. You will play the clarinet in our orchestra. We have two flautists, and until I begin inserting parts for the clarinet, you will also play the flute parts in the scores. Genevieve is currently first flautist, and I can tell you honestly that your musicianship is as good as hers, if not better. Like the other girls, you will practice every day for five hours after receiving lessons from the nuns in mathematics, Latin, history, and catechism. And you will obey the rules. Two hundred girls live in the Ospedale. But there are only forty of you in the elite orchestra and choir, and you must set an example. Do you understand?"

"Yes, Master."

"Luca will take you up to the dormitory, where you will be in the charge of Signora Marta."

"Thank you a million times over."

He put up his hand, then gestured toward the door.

I tried not to walk too quickly in my dress, which was difficult, excited as I was, and more than that, eager to escape the Master's presence.

"Nicolà," he called out, and I froze.

"Don't you want to know who Orpheus was?" He was already bent over his sheet music again, quill in hand.

I swallowed hard. "Yes, I do."

"He was the greatest musician that ever lived. He played a pipe made of reeds, like those that grow in the Lagoon. He liked to play as he walked, and his music was so beautiful it enchanted wild animals, and even the rocks in the fields, and animals and rocks alike followed him wherever he went. Can you imagine what that music must have sounded like?"

I shook my head.

"Neither can I," the Master said. "But I try to imagine whenever I compose music."

I was scarcely breathing at that point. All I could do was nod. He seemed to recall to whom he was speaking, and said, "Many of the girls here have nicknames, as you will discover. It is a shame yours cannot be Orpheus."

"Why not?"

"Because you're not a boy, of course."

"Of course," I agreed, and remembering to curtsy rather than bow, I hurried out the door.

7

The truth—the real truth—is that I was no Orpheus, and it had nothing to do with my gender. My mother had insisted that I could sing—or at least hum tunes—before I could speak. And that if I heard music, even some neighbor singing a scrap of song while doing his chores, or men regaling themselves while drinking wine, I would stop in my tracks to listen. When the tinsmith, in his ragged gray coat and floppy hat, made his rounds, he belted arias—off-key, often improvising nonsense lyrics—and I would follow him and sing along. "The problem with your boy," he joked to my mother, "is that he shows me up, because he never misses a note." So, yes, I had sung in the church choir, and soaked up the troubadours' ballads, and imitated the woodland birds, and I was indeed blessed with a musical memory (hearing a piece just once, I could repeat every note), but what I had dared not reveal to the Master was the special nature of my clarinet. *It* possessed unique powers that made *me* appear to possess great talent. Not surprisingly, this would turn out to be a mixed blessing.

The day my father presented me with the clarinet, the very first time I raised it to my lips, I was astonished to discover that I could play it proficiently. How was this possible, I asked myself, when I barely knew how to hold the instrument? I tried playing it again, but this time produced a mess of off-key notes. On my third attempt, my playing was again flawless—a snatch of organ music I

 28

had been humming that day. It took me an hour of trial and error before I solved the mystery: if I blew into the clarinet's embouchure while thinking of a tune, and hearing the notes in my head, my fingers would find the right holes and the tune would emerge perfectly. I had to concentrate hard, but it worked every time. If my concentration broke, the tune fell apart. As I grew adept, I attempted more complex music, including some of the Master's own concerti, and those of his great rival, Signor Albinoni, which I heard when a string quartet from Parma visited the church.

In short, I realized that my clarinet was enchanted. By what force or power, I couldn't imagine. I had grown up around people who believed in talismans, and not just the religious ones condoned by the Church, or the countless miracles performed by saints that I heard about during mass. My late grandmother, my father's mother, had possessed a blue amulet reputed to heal the sick. Supposedly it had revived a stillborn infant when placed on the child's chest and restored the sight of a blind girl. The day my grandmother died, the amulet disappeared, and my parents never did find it.

So enchantment was nothing new to me. But this was different: a musical instrument to whose magical properties I was a party. I doubted that Signor Agnetti knew of these properties or he would have guarded the clarinet more carefully, and certainly would not have allowed my father to carry it away so easily. I practiced daily, and after a while told myself that, despite the fact the clarinet was doing much of the work for me, each time I played a piece I learned more about how to breathe and blow, about fingering properly and employing complex dynamics. Like all clarinets at that time, mine had been fashioned to play in C or D major, and only with great effort did I learn to cross-finger all the sharps and flats, my fingers guided magnetically by the clarinet until I could work the eleven holes and three key pads in various combinations to produce eighteen keys from a low F to a high G sharp. It was as if the clarinet were teaching me how to play it—my breath, hands, and spirit absorbing the essence of the music, making it sound second nature to me. Imagine keeping your fingers on the keys of a mechanical clavichord—the Austrians called it a "player piano"—day after day, month after month, until eventually you could play on your own, on a regular keyboard. In short, if I had been truthful when the Master asked the identity of my teacher, I would have answered that it was the clarinet itself.

On Mazzorbo, it had not been difficult to conceal my secret. Outside of church, no one was much interested in music or musical instruments. I played the clarinet selectively, even around my family, and kept to the simplest pieces. One day when my sister Rhea picked it up and blew into it, I was terrified my secret would be revealed. But all that emerged from the clarinet was a dull squawk. She took a deep breath and tried again, with the same result.

I grew bold enough to ask Rhea to think of her favorite song while blowing into the embouchure. She had perfect pitch and was a far better singer than I.

"What good will that do?" she said.

"You may be surprised."

"Are you crazy?"

"Just try it. Please."

She put the clarinet to her lips and closed her eyes to concentrate, but this time all that emerged was a screech, and I breathed a sigh of relief.

Pushing the clarinet into my hands, she said angrily, "Just because I don't have your talent doesn't give you the right to mock me. It's cruel."

Even now, this is a painful memory, for I loved my sister and I couldn't explain what was behind my request and show her that no cruelty was intended. Any chance of doing so ended with her death.

As for my parents, they thought it a marvel that I could play at all. My father swore that one day I would take my clarinet out into the world and gain fame and fortune. My mother called it a miracle. And it was a miracle. I believe each of us is presented with one real miracle in life—if we can recognize it as such—and this clarinet with the mysterious powers was mine. I thought it best to keep those powers to myself until such time as I might truly need them and know how to employ them. The epidemic that swept Mazzorbo had hastened that moment, thrusting me out into the world and forcing me to live by my wits. The fact that I had nothing to fall back on made me guard my secret all the more vigilantly.

The Ospedale was not Mazzorbo; its residents were not simple peasants. Performing publicly with the city's finest orchestra, living among competitive, talented girls, I knew that keeping my secret was going to be far more difficult. When I added in the secret of my false identity, which the slightest misstep could reveal, my position felt even more precarious.

8

The dormitory for the elite orchestra, known as the *privileggiate di coro*, occupied the fourth floor of a brown building with tall yellow shutters and a terra-cotta roof that adjoined the church. The dining hall was on the third floor and practice rooms on the second. Two neighboring buildings comprised the greater part of the orphanage, housing the many children, some taking music lessons, others not, who were wards of the State. In yet another, much older building was the infirmary that was the original children's hospital from which the orphanage sprang. A hallway on the first floor of our building connected it to the nave of the church, and there were at least two hidden passageways on the upper floors linking the buildings, and rumor had it, a third, truly secret corridor known only to the Master, Luca, and Signora Marta, the *priora*, our official chaperone. Aldo must have known about it, too, as I discovered later.

The dormitory itself was not the airless, poorly lit space I expected. I had imagined a kind of drab convent: rows of narrow beds, clothing hanging on hooks, guttered candles, and a group of solemn girls whose saving grace was their music.

Instead, I followed Luca into a set of bright, lively rooms that were indeed "privileged," where several dozen high-spirited girls between the ages of eleven and seventeen, wearing white frocks and blue slippers, were bantering, reading, waxing violin strings, polishing lutes, annotating sheet music, and combing their hair before long mirrors. Those yellow shutters were open and the four large interconnected rooms were flooded with light. There was a ceiling mural of the sun ringed with angels in flight. The curtained beds were well spaced, each flanked by a chest of drawers and a night table with a pitcher and basin. Instrumentalists lived in the first two rooms, singers in the other two. Looking around at all the girls, and seeing that most of them were looking back at me, I wondered how I could possibly pull this off.

Signora Marta was waiting for me. She was an imposing woman who could have been forty or sixty. She always wore a stiff dress with a stiff white collar. Nearly as tall as Luca, she had long gray hair, parted down the middle, black unblinking eyes, and hands the width and weight of small shovels. Especially when they came down on the backside of one of the girls. She cursed and cuffed all of us in her charge, often cuffing us for the fact that we had cursed aloud.

Luca told her my name, shouted it, in fact—the first time I heard myself identified, like the other girls in the elite group, by the instrument I played: Nicolà dal Clarinetto, *Nicolà of the Clarinet*. With a stern glance at me, Luca left the room, and Signora Marta crossed her arms and inspected me from head to toe. Finally she gave me what I would learn was her customary greeting. "Wipe that smile off your face," she bellowed, whether you were smiling or not. And usually you weren't, but if you were, your smile disappeared.

I wondered at the fact that the laughter and chatter filling the rooms moments before hadn't seemed to bother her. And when two girls just a few feet from us began whispering, and Signora

33

Marta did not react, I realized she was nearly deaf. If you shouted like Luca, she could hear you; otherwise, she mostly acted upon what she saw. Which was why she often misread situations and reprimanded a girl who had done nothing wrong. As for our music, she never heard a note of it when she attended a performance. Only the timpanist, Agnes, occasionally penetrated her deafness. And it was Agnes who would tell me that Signora Marta had grown up in the orphanage, the abandoned child of a prostitute. Marta was a promising oboist, on the verge of joining the elite orchestra, when someone pushed her down a flight of stairs, causing her to hit her head and lose her hearing. Embittered ever since, she took out her rage on the girls of the orchestra, but always with an uncanny instinct for knowing just how far she could go without arousing the ire of the Master or the suspicions of the Governing Council, trustees of the Ospedale, appointed by the Doge, who were the Master's overseers. To the Council members, Signora Marta was someone who ran the dormitory smoothly and kept the girls out of scandals. When the latter occurred, she made sure they didn't become public.

Signora Marta led me to the bed I had been assigned, the second one in on the right-hand wall. My neighbors were Carita dal Cornetto, a small, silent girl with a sallow complexion, and Julietta della Tiorbo, a pretty brunette, my own age, who greeted me with a pleasant tilt of her head before returning to the book she was reading.

"Dinner is at six o'clock, Nicolà dal Clarinetto," Marta shouted. "Be in bed by nine o'clock. Make your bed at dawn. Bathe three times a week. Mind your manners. Attend morning

 34

mass and vespers Tuesday and Saturday. And say your prayers, for God is looking down on you."

The girls went back to their conversations, but no one came over to talk to me. I sat down on my bed holding my clarinet in my lap and kept my eyes politely lowered, the way my sister Alessandra used to. I tried to imagine how she would carry herself as a newcomer, the expression she would wear, the gestures she would make. Of all my sisters, she had the most poise. My mother used to say that she was the aristocrat of the family. Now she was just one of the dead, in a place where there were no aristocrats, no commoners, no one sick or poor and no one rich and robust, just a sea of blackness in which everyone became a shadow forever. Despite all I had been taught in church, and all my mother read to me from Scripture, I didn't believe in Heaven or Hell. When you left this life, you didn't go anywhere or experience anything. Put into the earth, you became one with it, like any other animal or plant. I didn't believe in God, either, for how could a God who was all-powerful, all-knowing, and infinitely merciful have so cruelly snatched away my gentle sisters and so many others for no reason at all? I would attend mass and vespers, but I planned to put wax in my ears so I didn't have to listen to the priests, and if the likes of Signora Marta believed that was heresy, for which you would be struck dead, so be it. If their God truly existed, and was so spiteful and uneasy that he would destroy a boy—or girl—who put wax in his ears, I wanted no part of the world he ruled.

When I glanced up from this jumble of thoughts, I saw Carita and Julietta looking at me sidelong. Then a beautiful blond girl on her way to bathe paused for a moment to smile at me, and say

"Welcome." At six o'clock Signora Marta rang a bell and all the girls trooped down one flight to the dining hall and took their assigned seats at two long tables. I looked for that blond girl, but she was at the far end of another table, with her back to me. Again I was between Carita and Julietta. Bowls of fish stew, baskets of white bread, and plates of olives and salted peppers were set before us. Marina the Prima Violinista, a tall, homely girl with a serious demeanor, led us in reciting the Lord's Prayer. After that, we were not allowed to speak during dinner. The clinking and scraping of forks and spoons were the only sounds.

Because the orchestra performed behind an iron grille, it had been impossible for me to view the musicians clearly during the one concert I attended. I only saw flashes of the girls' white blouses and their hair, and never an entire face but just a pair of lips or a cheek. Now that we were stationary, at close quarters, I began studying the girls seated around me, but the smell of the stew distracted and got the better of me. I ate with gusto, wolfing down chunks of fish and potato and mopping my bowl with bread. I had never tasted white bread, only black rye from the bakery on Mazzorbo. I told myself to be more ladylike, but I couldn't help it: the more I ate, the greater my hunger—as if my enforced fast of the previous days had caught up with me all at once. As I polished off the nearest plate of peppers, I caught a few girls watching me and exchanging glances. Marina glared at me until I put down my spoon and sat back, chewing softly and smiling at her, which seemed only to intensify her glare.

But that was the least of my worries, for soon after dinner the moment arrived that I had been dreading ever since I walked into the dormitory: I had to undress. Not only that, but I had to do so

 36

with the ease of a girl among other girls, not revealing I was a boy while trying to keep my eyes off all the girls undressing around me. It wasn't easy! I felt myself turn red as a beet, my nervousness obvious enough to prompt Julietta into breaking her silence. And she was so pretty I could barely avert my eyes when she unbuttoned her dress and pulled it over her head.

"You were hungry tonight, Nicolà," she murmured, turning down her bed.

I nodded and removed my own dress, and as quickly as possible dropped my nightdress over my head. I folded the dress and tucked it into the top drawer of my chest. I had expected the chest to be empty, but as if by magic it was already filled with stockings and shifts, underthings, a white frock and a blue one, and a pair of slippers. Opposite my bed, on a hook on the wall beside a dozen other blue woolen cloaks, there was one for me. Its distinctive red hood indicated that it belonged to a member of the elite orchestra. No other residents of the Ospedale could wear such a cloak.

After Signora Marta extinguished the candles along the walls, and loudly bade us good-night, I tucked my clarinet beneath my pillow and lay awake, feeling somewhat safer in the darkness. I marveled at how I had arrived at La Pietà, how the events of the previous week had alternated so easily between nightmare and dream. I began worrying that I could be expelled from the orphanage just as abruptly as I had entered it. Thus did my mind keep going round and round, but after such a long, stressful day, my weariness caught up with me. I drifted, lulled by the breathing of the girls around me, and had just crossed that hazy borderline into sleep when someone kissed me on the cheek. I thought I caught a whiff of hyacinth, but when I sat up, straining my eyes, I saw no one. The only sound I could hear was Carita snoring softly.

I laid my head back on the pillow, not sure if I had imagined this kiss or if it was real. If it did happen, I thought, which of my new companions had kissed me, and why?

II
The Orchestra

II

The Orchestra

1

At my first rehearsal in the Church of La Pietà, I tried to position myself in the second row, directly behind the blond girl who had smiled at me the previous evening, but with whom I had yet to exchange a word. Julietta had told me her name was Adriana dalla Viola. She said Adriana was one of her closest friends and offered to introduce me to her. There was something that drew me to Adriana, and it wasn't just her beauty, for there were any number of beautiful girls in the orchestra, including Julietta herself, who dressed and slept not four feet from me. Even in the brief time I had been around her, I saw that Adriana possessed a poise and calm I had seldom seen in an adult, much less in someone my own age. At any rate, my hope of standing close to her and speaking to her during a break was thwarted, and I was put in my place—literally—by Marina dal Violino, who was standing beside Adriana.

"You are in the back row," Marina said sharply, "the last and least among us with your strange instrument. You had better get there before the Master arrives. We never needed a clarinet before, and I doubt we need one now. You just take direction from Genevieve dal Flauto, the Prima Flautista, ask no questions, expect no favors, and hit the right notes."

Genevieve had black hair, knotted back severely, small ears, and brown hawk eyes that followed me to my place. Her expression was rigid. Her skin had an icy sheen, her lips were thin and white. She and Marina were sixteen years old, only two years my senior, but at that point in my life they felt far older.

A hush descended when we heard the Master's boots, followed by Luca's, on the stone steps that led to the mezzanine from a chamber behind the altar. The Master entered imperiously, scanning the orchestra without allowing his eyes to linger on any one of us. He was wearing a white robe with a gold collar and the white gloves, easily seen in dim concert halls, that he always wore when conducting. His red hair caught the light of the candles. Under his arm Luca was carrying a leather folder containing a stack of sheet music, which he distributed to us.

We were lined up, three deep, behind the iron grille, draped in crêpe, overlooking a wide hall where chairs would be set out for our performance the following night. The grille was intended to shield our identities, and in the sardonic words of Signora Marta, "to preserve whatever innocence you may still possess." After breakfast, setting up in a practice room, Julietta had filled me in on the intricacies of this issue while Carita frowned and averted her gaze, pretending to be deeply absorbed in polishing her cornet. Julietta was quite the coquette, and the rippling laughter with which she punctuated her conversation emerged naturally. A tradesman's son from the outer Lagoon, I had never been around girls like her.

"No matter what they say, I don't know that anyone gives much thought to virtue or innocence around here. Certainly not Marta or Luca. And when the Master puts his mind to such matters, it usually pertains to the chorus, especially the mezzo-sopranos," she said archly, "and not any of us. In short, despite all the rules heaped upon us, the only real rule is: 'Don't get caught,'" she added, tuning her tiorbo. "Meanwhile, you should know that when we reach the age of seventeen, we can be courted from the outside. We receive letters from gentlemen of the city requesting the company of a particular girl—with a chaperone, of course—based not on her appearance, which is supposedly unknown to them, but the quality of her playing. Even if it were true that our music seduces these men, would that make their intentions any purer?"

"Why are you filling her head with this rubbish?" Carita interjected. "She's only been here one day."

"She'll soon learn a lot more than that for herself," Julietta laughed. "We are given these letters by way of Marta, whose deafness, I should tell you, many of us doubt, having on rare occasions seen her react to sound. At any rate, we never know how many of these letters she actually receives, which ones she dispenses, which she withholds, and why." She lowered her voice. "And of course we don't know if, for a few coins, she doesn't provide a particular gentleman with a physical description of, say, Carita dal Cornetto."

"You can shut up now," Carita snapped.

"But some of us suspect these gentlemen know a good deal more about us than how we play our instruments," Julietta continued.

Carita grabbed her arm. "You had better watch what you say, Julietta, and who you say it to."

Both Julietta and I were taken aback by Carita's anger. Julietta was taller and stronger than Carita. She pulled her arm free and leaned in close to Carita. "Don't ever lay your hands on me again."

"One day you'll be sorry," Carita hissed, and stormed off.

As I spread out my sheet music on a stand, I could see that, despite her bravado, Julietta was shaken. It was obvious she had teased Carita before, but without drawing such a sharp response.

Though I knew it might be best to remain silent, I said to Julietta, "Why is she threatening you?"

"No matter. I'm not afraid of her, or the likes of her." She turned away, and proceeded to polish her tiorbo. Then, lowering her voice, and without a trace of her usual good spirits, she addressed my question without answering it: "You have only seen the surface of this place, Nicolà. It won't take you long to see what else is going on. Be careful who you trust."

All through our rehearsal at the church that afternoon, I kept one eye on the score and the other on the Master's baton. I missed none of my cues as we worked through his newest composition, a Concerto in F major. It was exhilarating for me to play with an orchestra, to be a part of this great synchronized mechanism whose volume the Master could raise or lower, whose dynamics he controlled, and whose colorations he could darken or lighten, all with a flick of his wrist. Even with the guidance of my clarinet, it was difficult for me to adjust at first, to hear the other musicians while also hearing myself; but I was grateful, for what might take a musician with a conventional clarinet several weeks, I managed in a few hours. This fact was not lost on some of the girls, every one of them with highly trained ears, after all, who cast approving glances my way. From what I heard later, they wondered if I was not a former conservatory student rather than the street musician I claimed to be, especially since I played such an exotic instrument. Information traveled fast in that small community, and within a couple of days my history—that is, the made-up version I had presented to Luca and the Master—was general knowledge. Those who speculated, out of genuine admiration or envy, decided the story could only be true if I was a sort of prodigy, able to play any score put before me with unerring accuracy.

"Have you ever heard of such a musician playing in the streets?" Genevieve dal Flauto sniffed to Marina dal Violino by the privy, knowing I was inside (having remembered to sit while peeing so my feet would be visible beneath the door). "And a girl, no less. I wonder where she really came from." These two had taken such an immediate dislike to me that I asked Julietta if they were hostile to all newcomers.

"Not all. Genevieve is threatened by you because the Master put you among the flutes, rather than the oboes, and obviously believes he can adapt the flute parts to your clarinet. Marina is mean-spirited, but not always so obvious about it. Something about you has gotten under her skin. But I like you, Nicolà. And I trust you." She embraced me, and I delighted in the warmth of her body against mine.

Despite that, and my pleasure in playing my clarinet at the rehearsal, I couldn't get Julietta's earlier words out of my head, and I wondered what it was she was warning me about at the Ospedale.

2

The following evening before dinner, Julietta and I were sitting on one of the stone benches in the Ospedale's courtyard. She had told me she had a surprise for me. A sea breeze blowing in from the Lido stirred the poplars. The marigolds and zinnias in flowerbeds shone like gems, yellow and gold, in the fading light. Deep shadows were lengthening on the cobblestones. Across the courtyard, through a low archway, I could see Bartolomeo Cattaglia, the cook, picking lettuce and radishes from the garden that supplied his kitchen. He was a broad-shouldered, ham-handed man with a grizzled beard and a curly mass of brown hair, graying around the ears. He had one eye and one good leg, the result of serving in the Republic's Navy in the Genoese and Sardinian Wars. He lost his eye to an arrow and his left leg below the knee to a cannonball. He himself had been a cannoneer on the admiral's flagship, but once he had to depend on a wooden leg, he found another way to serve by becoming a cook. That meant learning to transform the potatoes, onions, and salted fish that were the staples of seafaring galleys into tasty soups and stews. He was especially adept at preparing *sarde in saor*, the favored dish of Venetian sailors for centuries: layers of marinated sardines alternating with a paste of onions, raisins, and pine nuts. When he left the Navy finally, a highly decorated veteran, he took charge of the kitchens at the

Ospedale on the recommendation of the admiralty office. He set the place up like a ship's galley, pots and pans, highly polished, hooked to a broad beam, all utensils within reach, the butcher block scrubbed down daily with salt and sprinkled with olive oil, the oak floor swept clean, and the barrels in the storeroom neatly labeled. A number of cooks worked under him, feeding hundreds of girls, but Bartolomeo still tended to details like the vegetable garden himself, and he personally oversaw the meals served to the forty members of the *privileggiate di coro*. I was immediately drawn to him, I suppose, because, of all the men who worked at the Ospedale—Luca, Carmine, the thin high-strung porter, and of course the Master—Bartolomeo had far more in common with the men I had grown up around, my father and his fellow workers. Like my father, he came out of the laboring class, but had a much tougher background, having grown up in the back alleys of Santa Croce, notorious for its bare-knuckle boxers and knife fighters. It was no accident that the Navy conscripted most of its wartime sailors there. Ducal police sometimes rounded up a dozen men in a single tavern and sent them directly to the naval barracks on the Isola di San Pietro. Bartolomeo, however, was a volunteer, and proud of it.

In fact, my first interchange of sorts with him occurred that very evening, as he limped back to the kitchen, his black cane clicking loudly and a basket of vegetables tucked under his other arm. He paused at the sight of Julietta and me.

"Good evening, Julietta," he called out. "And you must be the new girl among the *privileggiate*."

"Yes, sir," I replied. "Nicolà dal Clarinetto."

"Welcome. Here is something for you both, to save for dessert." He reached into his pocket and produced two apricots, which he tossed to us in quick succession.

Julietta caught hers with both hands, but when mine sailed wide and high, I leaped up and dived for it, catching it with one hand and tumbling headfirst into the flowerbed. Julietta laughed with surprise when I jumped up, brandishing the apricot and brushing the dirt from my skirt, but Bartolomeo wasn't laughing. He took two steps toward us, squinting at me in the twilight.

"You're very athletic, Nicolà," he said.

And not at all ladylike, I thought with alarm. "Yes, sir," I said meekly.

"And how do you play the clarinet?" he said.

"She plays beautifully," Julietta said.

He nodded thoughtfully, turning away. "I shall look forward to hearing her."

How stupid of me to show off like that, I told myself; I should have let the apricot go, but I acted on blind instinct—as if I were still Nicolò Zen. The girls I'd known, like my sisters, were certainly capable of athletic play, of tussling, but a poised, well-mannered girl would resist diving into a flowerbed. Even if she wanted to, anyone who had worn a dress all her life would know instinctively that it was a bad idea. In short, I could disguise my voice all I wanted, but if I made mistakes like that, I would quickly be found out. It had taken very little to rouse the suspicions of a sharp-eyed man like Bartolomeo.

If Julietta suspected anything at all, she didn't let on. Instead, she said, "At last, Nicolà. Here is my surprise."

Still brushing my dress clean, I looked up as Adriana approached us from the dormitory entrance. My heart skipped a few beats, but I tried to conceal my excitement.

"My new friend here has been eager to meet you," Julietta laughed.

Adriana smiled at me. "And why is that, Nicolà dal Clarinetto?"

She said my new name in a singsong, trilling the *l*'s and *t*'s. For a moment, I was tongue-tied. Then I replied, inanely, "Because I am interested in the viola."

She pursed her lips. "And not in me? I hoped we would be friends—you and Julietta and I."

"Yes, of course, I hope so, too," I said.

"Good," she said, sitting down beside me. "Then tell me about yourself. Or have you already told Julietta everything?"

"Hardly," Julietta put in. "All I know is that she was playing in the streets for soldi when Luca invited her to audition."

"And where did you live?" Adriana asked.

"Here and there," I said. "Pensiones, boardinghouses— sometimes a bench in the Campo San Vio."

"That sounds dangerous," Adriana said. "And cold. But you look very healthy, despite all that."

"Maybe because of it," I lied, and it frightened me to hear what a fluent liar I had become.

"What do you mean?" Adriana said.

"I mean that maybe the experience made me stronger. You know, having to stay on my toes, persevering so I could eat."

"And you weren't afraid? I would have been."

"Only a little," I replied, thinking of my two dubious room-mates of the previous week, Giorgio and Filippo.

"All of us here have our stories," Adriana said, no longer smiling. "What is yours?"

I went on to tell the two of them how I had lost my family, including my two sisters and my supposed brother, Alessandro.

"That's terrible," Adriana said. "I'm so sorry."

"I'm sorry, too," Julietta said. "Then you were only performing in the street for a short time."

"I think one night would be quite enough," Adriana said.

"It wasn't so bad," I said, wanting to change the subject from myself. "I got lucky, after all. What about you, Julietta? How did you come to be here?"

"That is a long story. I'll tell you sometime."

At that moment, Carita appeared in the doorway to the dormitory.

"Uh-oh," Julietta murmured.

"Signora Marta will not appreciate your absence from dinner," Carita said.

"She sent you?" Julietta said.

"Of course. We've already finished our soup. She is not amused by your absence, so you had better hurry," she added before disappearing.

We rushed to the dining hall, and indeed, Signora Marta was very unhappy.

"You don't think you're going to dine with everyone else, do you?" she shouted as we prepared to take our seats. "You will stand at your places until the others are finished, and then go to bed. You will eat nothing. Anyone who gives you food will answer to me." She looked around the room. "Does everyone understand?"

 50

Adriana was on the other side of the room, but Julietta, beside me as usual, whispered, "Don't say anything. Just do as she says."

Later, I undressed hurriedly and slipped on my nightclothes. Every time I had to dress or undress, bathe, or use the toilet, I realized more fully what I had gotten myself into. It was not just the matter of concealing my sex; the girls of the Ospedale had habits my sisters could only have dreamed of, for the simple reason that my sisters had never enjoyed the luxury of brushing their hair with a fine-bristled brush until it shone, or applying a lavender cream on their faces and hands to keep them soft, or whitening their teeth and freshening their breath with fennel water and crushed cloves. Sometimes as I learned about hair, and facial balms, female clothing, and the like, I rued the fact I was not gaining knowledge of the clothing and accoutrements a boy in higher station would wear. For example, instead of learning how properly to polish a pair of boots, I was practicing tying my hair back with a ribbon without standing before a mirror. Though the chances of my becoming a gentleman who moved in society were very slim, the chances of my doing so as a young lady were nil. Why I felt I had the luxury of ruminating on such matters I don't know. At that moment, I had no business fretting about the future when I could barely deal with my present circumstances.

Like Julietta, from whom I kept trying unsuccessfully to avert my eyes as she sat not six feet from me brushing her long hair, her breasts visible through the thin shift that had replaced her dress. She had fuller breasts than most of the other girls, some of whom—like me!—were flat-chested. She caught my glance, and smiled, offering me her brush, but I shook my head.

I was very hungry. But only when we had gotten into bed did I remember the apricot in the pocket of my dress, which was hanging on the wall at the foot of my bed. I waited for several minutes after Signora Marta had extinguished the candles before slipping out of bed and retrieving the apricot. But no sooner had I gotten under my blanket again than I heard a match struck as Carita lit a candle, blinding me as she thrust it toward me and shouted, "Nicolà is eating in bed."

I had never hit a girl, but I had to restrain myself from jumping up and slapping her. I rationalized that I would be doing this as a girl, after all, but the moment passed, and with it any hope of escaping the wrath of Signora Marta, who appeared at my bedside, flushed and furious. After snatching away the apricot, she grabbed my shoulder.

"Who gave you this?" she shouted, shaking me.

I wouldn't answer.

"Who?"

"Signor Cattaglia."

"You dare to mock me?"

"He gave it to me, before dinner."

"It's true," Julietta piped up. "I saw him do it."

"Who gave you permission to speak, Julietta?"

"You can ask him, signora," I said. "I swear to it."

"You swear? You can swear to Luca tomorrow, you liar. You'll learn to follow the rules here, or you'll be out in the street again."

She stormed off, and as Carita blew out her candle and pulled up her covers, Julietta hissed, "You bitch. I hate you."

"I warned you to watch your tongue, Julietta."

"Go to hell."

"Shut up, the both of you," someone cried from out of the darkness.

It took me a while to fall asleep, not so much because I was agitated over Signora Marta's threats as the fact that I was hungry. I thought she was more bluster than substance, and after all the death I had experienced the previous week, her threats felt hollow. I did console myself with the notion that somehow, in some way, I would take my revenge on Carita.

In the morning, I was awakened by a pair of angry voices. Drowsy, I imagined for a moment that Julietta and Carita were still arguing. Then I saw that it was Signora Marta and Carmine, the porter, beside Julietta's bed. The bed was neatly made, and her bedside chest had been emptied. Her tiorbo was gone, too.

"How could she have just disappeared?" Signora Marta demanded.

"All the doors were locked," Carmine replied in his hoarse, squeaky voice, "except the front door, and I never left my post."

An hour later, Adriana and I waited outside the practice rooms, with another of her close friends, Prudenza dal Violette. Prudenza was a slight girl with black hair and brown eyes and a ready smile.

"Julietta's run away," she observed.

"I only wish that were the case," Adriana murmured, sending a chill through me. "Meet me in the courtyard after rehearsal," she whispered in my ear.

3

Waiting for Adriana, watching the shadows creep across the roof-tops, I kept thinking that, just twenty-four hours before, Julietta had sat beside us on that same bench. I could still hear her voice and see the wind ruffling her hair.

When Adriana appeared, she looked distracted. It was cool out, despite the bright sunlight, and though we were both wearing our cloaks, she had also wrapped a shawl around her neck. Still not accustomed to female clothing, I had not thought to take one myself from the large chest in the dormitory common room where sweaters, hats, and gloves were also available to us. I wondered how girls could stand to wear dresses when they offered so little protection from the cold dampness that rose from the canals. My legs and privates grew numb after just a few minutes outside.

"Julietta is the third girl to disappear," Adriana said. "With the other two, there were legitimate explanations, which may or may not have been true. But that is not the case with her."

"Three disappearances? When did the others disappear?"

"November. You said Julietta told you that all is not as it seems here."

"She didn't say why."

"Because she probably knew no more than I do."

"But if she didn't run away, what's happened to her?"

 54

She shrugged. "I only know that she isn't the type to run, un-less she was very frightened."

"Of Signora Marta?"

"No, no. I mean, frightened for her life." She paused. "You're new here, Nicolà, but that's not the only reason I trust you. There's something else about you. Julietta noticed it, too."

Yes, I thought. I only wish I could tell you what it is.

"Think about who was threatening Julietta," she went on.

"Carita. But why?"

"The second girl who disappeared like this was Lutece dal Cornetto. Just two months ago."

"Cornetto?"

"Yes. Carita replaced her as Prima Cornettista. We were told that relatives had come for Lutece. A wealthy cousin from Man-tua who discovered she was here and took her home."

"Who told you?"

"Luca. He announced it to all of us at dinner, as if it were a happy event."

"And no one saw her leave?"

"Only Genevieve. She told us her departure had come about very quickly. Julietta and I didn't believe her. Both of us knew that Lutece was not like that. She had many friends and would never have left without a word to them. And she never men-tioned any connection to Mantua. As for Genevieve, at the time I thought it was a coincidence."

"That she was the last to see her?"

"No, that she was also the only one to say farewell to the first girl to leave suddenly, Silvana dal Basso."

"And where did she go?"

"Naples, supposedly, for a reunion with her long-lost brother, a ship's captain. Luca made no announcement about her. After all, it didn't seem so unusual at the time. Girls come and go, it's the nature of the place. They're married off to suitors, or they take positions in other orchestras, or are hired as music teachers. But until Silvana, they always said goodbye. In fact, there would often be a small gathering, with tea and cakes, to send them on their way." She shook her head. "I'm frightened, Nicolà."

I took her hand and tried to hold it as I imagined another girl would, though I wasn't sure I got that right. "There are things you're not telling me," I said.

She looked surprised.

"I can see it in your face."

She squeezed my hand. "I *can* trust you. It's like this: Julietta told me a terrible secret. I didn't believe it at first, not because I doubted her, but because it just doesn't seem possible. She said that Aldo and one of the girls—one among us—were taking other girls to the wine cellar. They would give the girls wine, and one thing would lead to another . . . against the girls' better judgment, perhaps against their will. Afterward, Aldo would be able to threaten and blackmail them into doing more of the same, or worse."

I tried to take all this in. "Aldo? Which of the girls would help him do such things?"

"Julietta didn't know who it was."

"And this is what she thought happened to the two girls who disappeared suddenly?"

"She didn't say that. Maybe there is no connection. But it's

 56

possible their encounters with Aldo were only the beginning of their troubles. In this city every kind of vice is close at hand. You must know that, Nicolà." Adriana looked up and scanned the windows of the Ospedale that overlooked the courtyard on three sides. "Don't you feel as if someone is watching us?"

I hadn't, until that moment. "Even if they are, they can't hear us." I glanced up and thought I did see someone in the shadows beside a curtain in a fourth-floor window. Your imagination is getting away from you, I told myself. "Do you think it's true about the wine cellar?" I asked.

Adriana hesitated. "I do. Because of something I myself saw. One night several weeks ago, when everyone was asleep, I heard someone crossing the dormitory. With the candles extinguished, it becomes pitch-dark, as you know. But I caught a glimpse of her face: it was Genevieve dal Flauto. For a moment, I thought she might be going to the privy. But she wasn't wearing a nightdress; she had on a dress and a coat. When she reached the door, I saw someone waiting for her. He held a small candle down low, so as not to illuminate his own face, but I could make it out in the darkness. It was Aldo. Beside him was another girl—all I could make out in the shadows was her long hair. I couldn't sleep after that. Two hours later, just before first light, Genevieve returned to the dormitory with Bellona dal Cembalo. Have you met Bellona?"

"No. I saw her at the rehearsal."

"I thought she must have been the second girl. Some of the girls say she had a wild life before she arrived here. That she has been with men, and learned the worst about them."

"Does the Master know any of this?"

"I doubt it. Anyway, he is too involved in his own affairs—

57

with Anna del Coro, the mezzo-soprano, to be precise. There is nothing particularly hidden about that, at least here in the Ospedale."

"Julietta hinted as much."

"The Master often travels alone with Anna, and her sister Rosa. Don't look so surprised, Nicolà. That's the reason most of the girls have paid little attention to these other doings. They expect secrecy and intrigue in this place. After all, nearly everyone's origins are secret." She paused. "Including my own. I've only shared mine with Julietta. Would you like to know how I came to be here?"

4

"My mother's name was Heléne Manzone," Adriana said. "I don't know who my father was. My mother was from Modena. She fell ill, and when she realized she wasn't going to recover, she sent me here. One month later, she died. I was five years old. Her parents were dead, she had broken off with the rest of her family, so there were no relatives she could have left me with. They were all poor people, but my mother and I lived in a fine apartment in Modena. There were two servants, one of whom, Consuela, looked after me most of the time. My mother didn't work, but she was frequently out. I couldn't understand how she could afford such a life until I was older and realized she must have been a courtesan." She looked away. "She could have been with a number of men, but I would like to think she was one man's mistress. A wealthy merchant, perhaps, who may have been my father. Whoever he was, I never met him. We seldom had visitors, and never men. I was only a child, but I sensed that she was very cautious about who she saw and spoke with. That's why I believe she had a single lover. Only once, when I was out with my mother in her carriage, did I see her with the man I thought that could be. It was just for an instant, on a street of high white houses and shade trees in Modena. My mother told me to wait in the carriage while she went into one of those houses. I watched a footman admit her. Through a window beside the door I could look into a well-furnished drawing room. Suddenly my mother appeared, crossing the room. A man met her midway. He was tall, dark-haired, wearing a blue dressing robe. But he had his back to the window, and I never saw his face. They exchanged words, he disappeared, and before I knew it, she was back beside me in the carriage. When I asked her who the man was, she was surprised. She grew agitated, asking me what I had seen, exactly, but after I told her, she calmed down.

"'He is a friend,' she said.

"'Is he also my father?'

"'Why do you say that?'

"'Well, my father must be somewhere.'

"'He is far away from here.'

"'Will I ever meet him?'

"'I feel sure you will, someday.'

"That was the only conversation on the subject I remember. She got sick soon afterward, and then this became my home. I showed some musical talent on the lute and the pianoforte, and they gave me lessons on the viola. I was admitted to the *privileggiate di coro*. Most of the other girls don't know their parentage. You're one of the lucky ones." She stopped herself. "I'm sorry, Nicolà. I wasn't thinking."

"It's all right. For a long time I was lucky."

"Do you know why the Ospedale is so well kept? Why we have fine linens and the best food?"

"I know it is supported by the State."

She smiled. "True, but the Doge is only generous up to a point. After which the Master must rely on his musical patrons. It happens that the most generous of these are motivated by more than music." She leaned closer to me. "You see, there have been girls here who were the daughters of princes and dukes. A few years ago, Angela dal Violino discovered she was the daughter of the Duke of Parma. He acknowledged her and took her away. Another girl, a contralto named Magdalena, received an anonymous letter informing her that her father was the Prince of Naples. Sometimes we see these rich and powerful men who come to visit the Master and make their donations, and we try to guess if anyone is connected to them by birth. Prudenza knows her mother was a prostitute, but one day it was whispered in her ear that her father was a Swedish count who for a time lived in Venice. She waits for him to come. Me, I've stopped waiting. I have looked hard at these men, trying to find a resemblance, some similarity to my own features. I doubt my father, whoever he is, knows I am here. In fact, I'm not so sure my mother ever told him of my existence."

"Why wouldn't she tell him?" I asked naïvely.

"Because of who he was. Perhaps a member of the clergy, like the Master—although I don't fancy myself the daughter of a priest. Or a married man who decided to break off with her. Who knows?"

"You'll find him one day."

She shrugged. "Or perhaps I'll discover he is someone I don't want to find."

5

The following night, for the first in my life, I was thrilled to perform in public before a large audience. Among the three hundred people in attendance were some of the city's wealthiest, most powerful citizens, eager to hear the début of the Master's latest concerto, conducted by Vivaldi himself. From our screened perch in the mezzanine, the members of the orchestra could study the audience freely. The ladies wore flowing gowns and long silk shawls and the brightly colored, feathered headdresses that were in fashion. Their jewelry glittered beneath the chandeliers. I could smell their perfumes wafting upward as they cooled themselves with hand-painted fans depicting dragons and leviathans that our trading vessels had brought back from the Orient. The gentlemen wore black dress coats and ruffled white shirts. Their wigs were powdered pale blue. I recognized the Archbishop in his gold-trimmed cassock; and the renowned opera singer Chiaretta Fanosa, draped in pearls; and the Doge's stern younger brother, Admiral Cornaro, who had become famous for a battle off the coast of Sicily in which he sank half the Sardinian fleet and lost an eye. Coming from where I did, my sudden proximity to such people was dizzying. The girls around me were relaxed, tuning their instruments and studying the sheet music. They had performed publicly many times, so none of this was new to them.

All afternoon I had been thinking about Julietta and Adriana, but when the Master raised his baton and signaled us to begin, I cleared my head and threw myself into the music. This concerto, in B-flat major, did not feature a particular soloist, on string or wind instrument, but there were two violin solos, assigned of course to the Prima Violina, and four brief, energetic flute solos. In rehearsal, the latter had been played by the Prima Flautista, Genevieve dal Flauto. But as we took our places in the mezzanine, Luca had come to the flute section and informed us that the Master wanted me, Nicolà Vitale, to play the fourth of these solos on my clarinet.

Genevieve was furious. "There must be some mistake," she said.

"No mistake." Luca scowled.

"But she's not even a flautist—and she's only been here for a week."

"Just do as you're told," he snapped. "And you, Nicolà: don't disappoint the Master."

Genevieve's cheeks flushed. She bit her lip. I thought she was going to burst into tears. But that wasn't her way. When Luca was gone, she grabbed my arm, and digging her nails in, whispered, "You'll pay for this."

"It wasn't my idea," I said, squeezing her wrist until she released my arm.

She seemed surprised by my strength. "You've been looking for trouble since you arrived here, and now you've found it."

Carmona dal Flauto, the second flautist, who had not previously acknowledged my existence, looked at me with disdain. "I hate you, too," she said.

I wanted to tell them both off, but I held my tongue and

turned away, trying to understand why the Master would order me to play a solo. Mean-spirited as they were, these girls were right: I was green, barely settled in. Why would he want to test me at this point?

I'd had only a few moments to study the solo, near the end of the third movement. I saw at once that, though written for flute, it was easily playable on the clarinet. When its moment arrived, the other instruments broke off and the Master's eyes alighted on me, and the silence was so profound that I reminded myself to breathe. And above all else to concentrate, to focus on each note as I played it, so that my clarinet might do its work. The Master nodded and I launched into the solo, a rapid crescendo, *allegro con brio*, that restated the opening bars of the movement and lasted about thirty seconds, which felt like an hour. My concentration did not waver and my clarinet did not fail me: I hit no wrong notes, I shaded the dynamics properly, and I added a depth on the lower octaves that was not possible on a flute. As the rest of the orchestra started up again, I played into the flow without a hitch and caught a small smile on the Master's face before he turned away.

When we finished, we received a sustained ovation, which grew louder when the Master took his bows. But Genevieve was still seething. The fact I had played well further incensed her.

After we returned to the dormitory, Adriana took me aside, where no one could hear us.

"Congratulations," she said. "I feel sure the Master is going to make you the principal soloist in the flute section."

"No, it's much too soon. One solo in my first concert—and not even on the flute!"

"He doesn't care about things like that. He operates according to what he last heard, and what his instincts tell him. I've seen it before. He promoted Prudenza after only two concerts."

"And Genevieve?"

"She will become Seconda Flauto. And Carmona will be Tertia."

"And they will hate me even more."

"Genevieve hates everyone, except Marina."

I shook my head. "I hope you're wrong about this."

She kissed my cheek. "Then you should not have played so flawlessly, my friend."

6

That night, after tucking my clarinet under my pillow, I was too excited to fall asleep. The applause was still echoing in my ears. But I also had a sense of foreboding. Each day at the Ospedale had been more disturbing than the last: the stories I had heard, the envy and hostility I had felt. My previous life had in no way prepared me for this one. The one-room schoolhouse and tiny church choir on Mazzorbo had been the extent of my education. Since all the children were poor, with no expectation of advancement, there was little sense of competition at either place. "If you can talk, you can sing," our priest, Father Michele, used to say. The difference between his choir and the *privileggiate di coro*—or even the midlevel *coro* at the Ospedale—was enormous. Despite my initial hopes, I wasn't sure now that I could ever feel comfortable at the Ospedale—and my disguise was the least of it.

Soon after I fell asleep, someone whispered in my ear, "Wake up."

I sat up, and there was Aldo, kneeling at my bedside, grinning. His milky eyes looked even whiter in the darkness.

"Good evening, Nicolà." He leaned closer. "Or should I say, Nicolò."

He sensed my panic and his smile widened.

"Oh yes, I'm on to you," he said.

"What are you talking about?"

"I have to hand it to you. It must be difficult to wear a dress, learn to curtsy, remember to sit down when you pee. Though you do forget sometimes, you know."

How could he know that? I thought.

"I don't need to see you in the privy," he went on. "I can read the sounds. The rustle of clothes, the piss hitting from higher up. It's easy for me."

"Go away or I'll call Marta."

"Call her. It won't take her long to determine which of us is telling the truth." He leaned a few inches closer. "But I have a better idea: you give me something I want and your secret remains safe."

I was wide awake now, but felt as if I had stumbled into a nightmare. "What could I possibly give you?"

"Adriana," he replied with a crooked smile. "Bring her to the wine cellar tomorrow night and I'll forget everything I know about you."

"Go to hell."

"Maybe I will. But if you don't bring her, I'll go to Luca and you'll be sent packing."

"What if I speak to them first?"

"They won't believe you. And after she hears from me, Marta will check beneath your little dress and confirm that you're an impostor and a liar. In no time, you'll be back on the street. Don't try to warn Adriana off, because I'll know about it. Tell her you're taking her to Julietta. She trusts you. Knock four times at the door to the wine cellar and leave immediately. Don't look back at Adriana. And don't say another word now." He backed away into the darkness. "Eleven o'clock. Sleep well, Nicolò."

7

I felt sick the next morning. I saw Adriana across the room at breakfast. She smiled at me, but I didn't have the chance to speak with her. The entire string section—violins, violas, bass viols— were sitting at the same table. When they were finished eating, Marta ushered them downstairs to a large rehearsal room. They would spend the next four hours there while I was assigned to a practice room with Prudenza, playing the violette, and a bassoon- ist named Lucia, a shy girl with flushed cheeks who was reputed to be the daughter of a Milanese prince imprisoned in Austria. We had been told to play two of the Master's sonatas as well as a trio by Albinoni. But we had barely begun when Luca entered the room looking grim.

"The Master wants to see you," he said to me.

"Now?"

"Yes, now. You two play on without her."

I was certain Aldo had turned me in; after discovering some other means of getting at Adriana, he wanted me out of the way.

When I entered his office, the Master was by the window, gazing at the sailboats on the canal. He was wearing a white shirt, ink-stained at the cuffs, and blue trousers. As usual, his desk was littered with sheet music. His yellow cat, Giacomo, was curled up on an ottoman. "Good morning, Nicolà," he said pleasantly. "Please, sit. So how do you like life at the Ospedale?"

This wasn't what I had expected. It took me a moment to gather my wits. "Of course I like it, Master."

I obviously didn't sound convincing, for he stepped out of the sunlight and walked over to me. He got so close that I could see his left eye was a paler blue than his right, and his hair more orange than red. "You're sure?" he said.

"Yes, Master."

"Good. Because I am making you my Prima, Clarinetto, first soloist in the flute section. Beginning today."

I was both relieved and terrified.

"I was impressed by your performance last night," he continued. "Your confidence. Your feel for the music. And, most of all, your ability to adapt the flute line to the clarinet. It was what I was hoping you could do."

"Thank you."

"You learned a great deal from those birds in the forest you mimicked," he added dryly.

Again I was caught off guard, for Adriana had told me he rarely displayed a sense of humor. Despite my nervousness, I forced a smile.

He handed me some sheet music. "You have provided me an inspiration. I am converting the flute solos in my new concerto into solos for the clarinet. I can widen the octave range and expand the solos. No small thing. The flute parts will remain, to be played by our two flautists. When a piece calls specifically for a flute solo, the Seconda Flautista will play it. But that is not your concern. What do you think: are you pleased?"

"Of course, Master." In fact, the notion that I had in any way inspired Antonio Vivaldi was beyond my comprehension just then.

"Good," he said. "We will be performing this concerto next Sunday, at San Stefano. It contains seven clarinet solos of varying length. Study them. Prepare yourself."

My throat was closing up. "I won't disappoint you."

"Good luck, then," he said, petting Giacomo and returning to his desk.

As I walked down the long, low-lit corridor from his office, past a succession of doors, one of them opened and someone stepped out behind me.

"What were you doing in there?" Aldo demanded. Up close, I better appreciated his size: a head taller than me, maybe twenty kilos heavier, with those big, heavy hands I had noted the first time I saw him.

Nevertheless, with all the defiance I could summon, I said, "I told you to go to hell."

He took my arm and twisted it. "Don't ever say that to me again."

I pulled free. "The Master called me in. He's promoting me to Prima Clarinetto."

Aldo laughed. "That's a good one, pretty boy. Because if you don't do what I told you, you'll never play with the orchestra again, as Prima or anything else. You won't even be allowed to sweep the floors. Eleven o'clock," he hissed, disappearing through another door.

My practice session seemed interminable. Despite the honor bestowed on me by Antonio Vivaldi himself, my heart wasn't in the music. Afterward, Prudenza asked me what was wrong, but I put her off. I had decided I couldn't trust anyone except Adriana. All afternoon I was miserable, trying to plot out my best course of action. But every scenario I concocted ended badly. I did not doubt that Aldo would carry through on his threat, and that left me with the narrowest of choices: because I would never put Adriana in danger, I could either quietly accept expulsion from the Ospedale or put myself in danger in order to expose Aldo so he could no longer threaten Adriana or any other girl.

I chose the latter, for though I knew I was likely to fail, it was better than doing nothing. Aldo was blind, but I felt I was truly operating in the dark when I came up with a plan.

At dinner I noticed that Marina and Genevieve looked at me with even more hostility than usual, but also with a certain smug self-satisfaction. I had always been suspicious of them, and now I wondered if they might somehow be in league with Aldo. Or if Carita, a few feet away in her bed, had eavesdropped on my conversation with Aldo the previous night and reported it to Genevieve. As for Adriana, she left the dining room early and was already asleep when I retired to the dormitory. With all the other girls filing in and readying themselves for bed, I couldn't wake her up and have a private conversation. In fact, I concluded it was better that she not know what I was about to do.

After Signora Marta extinguished the candles, I feigned sleep until I was sure Carita's snores were genuine. Then I put my dress back on and got under the covers and waited until quarter to eleven. As I slipped out of bed, I was sweating and my mouth was dry. I draped my cloak over my shoulders, fastening the button at the throat and pulling the hood up over my head. Then I picked up my shoes and made my way to the door on tiptoe.

Marta made her rounds of the dormitory twice each night: first, at ten o'clock, an hour after bidding us good-night, and a second time at no fixed hour, and thus completely unpredictable. (My theory was that it corresponded to her nocturnal visit to the privy.) In short, I knew I might run into her at any moment.

Once out the door, I put on my shoes and walked down the hallway to the wide landing at the head of the main stairway. I could either take those stairs to the lobby, where Carmine the porter sat by the street door, or I could go to the end of the hall and descend a small, dark stairwell that led directly to the basement. The latter seemed the safer choice, its only drawback the fact that Marta's quarters were directly off of it on the second floor. I proceeded carefully as my eyes adjusted to the semidarkness. At the third-floor landing, I heard heavy footfalls—like a man's boots—in a nearby corridor. I backed up against the wall, holding my breath, but the footfalls stopped abruptly. Continuing on, I was soon outside Marta's quarters. Beneath her door there was a band of light. Either she was awake, reading her Scripture, or asleep beside a burning candle. Gripping the front of my cloak so it wouldn't rustle—in case she wasn't deaf—I walked as lightly as I could past her door and down the remaining stairs. The stairwell grew dimmer until finally I was engulfed by darkness, as if I had descended into a deep well.

In the basement, myriad doors led to storage rooms, and instruments of every sort lined the walls, from cembalos to stringless lutes. A single taper was lit, beside a narrow door. I opened it and walked down a steep set of stairs to a subbasement where, in the bowels of the Ospedale, at the end of a short L-shaped hallway, a final door of thick oak planks led to the wine cellar.

I pulled my hood as far forward as I could, concealing my face completely, took a deep breath, and knocked four times. The door opened and Aldo's large pale face appeared. He cocked his ear, listening for retreating footfalls down the hallway, but there was only silence.

"Nicolà followed my instructions," he muttered, "but she must be quite fleet-footed. Welcome, Adriana."

I kept my lips sealed; with his acute sense of hearing, unless I whispered, he would surely be able to distinguish my voice from Adriana's. My scent was another matter, and he obviously intended to test it: before opening the door, he stuck his thick, blunt nose inches from my face and sniffed.

"You don't smell the way I expected," he said.

"No?" I whispered as sweetly as I could. "Then I'll go."

"You won't," he said, taking my arm firmly and pulling me into the wine cellar.

It was like a cave: walls and floor of heavy stone, the ceiling beams rough-hewn. The air was dank and cold. Several candles were burning, but the light was dim. Moldy wine casks lined the walls. A broken crucifix, speckled with bloodred paint, was hung on the far wall, just beneath the low ceiling. Two chairs were set face to face in the center of the room beside a large candle.

"Take off your cloak," Aldo said, "and sit down."

It was then I saw we weren't alone. A man in a black cape and hat was standing in the corner, behind the last cask.

I hesitated, but Aldo firmly guided me to one of the chairs. "I'll get you a cup of wine," he said.

Reluctantly I removed my cloak, my eyes riveted on the man in the shadows. He took a step forward, but I still could not see his face. I heard a gurgling sound on my right as Aldo filled a wooden cup. He emptied it in a single gulp and refilled it.

When I sat down, the large candle illuminated me fully. With that, the man in the shadows broke his silence.

"You told me her hair was yellow," he said to Aldo.

"It is," Aldo protested.

"Maybe if you're blind," the man said acidly.

"What goes on here?" Aldo demanded, putting down the wine cup, and grabbed my shoulder. With his other hand, he tried to feel the contours of my face. I pulled away from him, and for a split second saw Aldo's visitor clearly as he stepped into the light: a middle-aged man with a craggy face, gray beard, long nose, and close-set eyes. Suddenly the man laid hands on me, pinning my arms behind my back.

"Let me see her," the man said through his teeth, and before I could move, Aldo ripped my dress right down the front, exposing my nakedness.

"Hey!" I cried out.

"My god," the man shouted, releasing my arms. "She's a boy!"

"What!"

"You're a fool and a liar, Aldo," the man growled, beating a retreat to the door. "And you'll pay for this."

Aldo immediately understood what had happened. "It's you!" he cried, lunging at me with outstretched arms.

I jumped from the chair, avoiding his grasp. "Don't touch me, you pig. Did you really think I would bring Adriana here?"

Aldo was livid, but didn't lose sight of his objective, which was to corner me. Just as with every other room in the Ospedale, he had the wine cellar mapped out in his head to the last detail. It was unnerving to watch him move about as if he could see. No matter how much I backpedaled, ducked, or skipped this way and that, he kept closing in on me.

"Adriana's not here," he said, "but you are. And I'm going to give you a beating you'll never forget."

"I'll tell Luca what you've been doing down here."

"Luca!" he laughed. "That's a good one. Don't forget to tell him who you really are."

That laugh took the heart out of me. I realized that, even if I managed to get out of that cellar in one piece, the repercussions of my having come there would be dire. I had hoped that, by threatening Aldo with exposure, I could preserve my secret and remain at the Ospedale. What was I thinking? Even with my limited knowledge of the world, I ought to have realized that only a fool would attempt to blackmail a blackmailer.

Aldo had finally pushed me up against the wall, and dropping his shoulder, charged forward and knocked the wind out of me. Then he came at me with his fists. Having been around rough men, my father had taught me the rudiments of defending myself: *Keep your hands up and wait for an opening.* Aldo swung wildly at first, and I was able to avoid the blows, but then he caught me on the ear and hit me in the mouth, cutting my lip. He reared back to punch me again, but tried packing so much into it that he tottered, slightly off-balance, and I saw my opening: I landed a punch squarely on his jaw, so hard that I thought I had broken my knuckles. I followed this with a kick to his shin, and another to his groin that doubled him over, but didn't stop him. Cursing loudly, he started swinging again for my head. It was terrifying to fight someone who was blind, yet could move so swiftly and strike blows so precisely. Every time I attempted to circle around to the door, he cut me off. If he was able to pounce on me again, I knew he wouldn't let go until he had really hurt me. So, lowering my head, I took him by surprise, bolting right past him and pushing one of the chairs into his path. When he stumbled over it, I picked up the other chair and swing it as hard as I could, catching him on the shoulder and the head.

Staggered, but staying on his feet, he shouted, "You little bastard," and lunged at me.

I ran to the door and threw it open and plunged into the hallway, right into the hands of someone who lifted me off the ground.

"Where do you think you're going?" he growled, shaking me so hard I thought he would crack my spine.

It was Luca.

All I managed to say was, "I can't explain, but thank god you're here, signor."

Luca ignored me and glared at Aldo. "What goes on here?" he demanded.

"He's an impostor," Aldo shouted.

"He?"

"Look at him."

It took Luca a moment to understand. He tore my dress open completely. "Who the devil are you?"

"Let me go," I said, trying to break free.

"Look what you did to me," Aldo shouted, feeling blood trickling from a gash in his temple. "I'll kill you."

"You'll shut your mouth," Luca snapped. "Who else knows about this?"

Aldo hesitated. "Nobody."

Luca squeezed my arm and shook me again. "Does anyone know you're down here?"

I shook my head.

"Speak!"

"No."

"What is your real name?"

"Nicolò."

"Very clever. Well, Nicolò, you're going right back where I found you."

"I want to see the Master," I said.

"You've got nerve," Luca said, shoving me back into the wine cellar and slamming the door behind us.

"Have you any idea what you've done?" he demanded. "Did you set out to make fools of us?"

"No, signor."

"Sit down," he said, righting one of the chairs, "and tell me what you could possibly want to say to the Master."

My mind was racing. "That I'm sorry."

"Sorry you were caught out?"

"No. I'm sorry I broke the rules and left my bed."

"The rules? You should never have had a bed here!"

"I am sorry that I deceived him, and you, pretending to be a girl. The truth is I am an orphan. I did lose my family. When you found me in the street, I was cold and hungry with nowhere to go."

"Am I supposed to feel bad for you, after all your deceptions? Why did you come down here tonight?"

I glanced at Aldo, who was itching to get at me again. "Because he threatened me."

"What?"

"He said if I didn't bring Adriana dalla Viola, he would expose me."

Luca turned to Aldo. "You knew he was a boy?"

"No, he's lying. He came here to drink wine. I caught him."

"That's not true."

"Why would Aldo want you to bring Adriana?" Luca asked.

"So he could assault her."

"That's a fantastic accusation."

"And he would have turned her over to a man who was hiding here."

"What man?" Luca said.

"He had a gray beard, an ugly face."

"He's a liar!" Aldo cried.

"I tricked Aldo," I went on, "to protect her, so he started beating me."

"Why would I believe anything you say?" Luca said with disgust. "You lied to me the first time we spoke, did you not?"

"Yes," I admitted.

"And you've done nothing but lie since you entered the Ospedale. Your very presence here is based on a lie. And you're lying now."

"I'm not."

"I've had enough of this," Luca said, hauling me up by the collar of my dress.

He dragged me to the door and threw it open, and to our astonishment, Signora Marta was crouched outside, obviously peering through the keyhole and listening.

So she could hear! I thought.

"Marta, what are you doing?" Luca said.

Without a word, she slapped me across the cheek, so hard that it stung for the next hour, which was so chaotic and frightening that I barely noticed.

She put her face inches from mine and shouted, "You're a disgrace!" Then she whacked my head, and would have continued hitting me had Luca not stopped her.

"Let's just get him out of here," he said.

As we climbed the stairs, she in front, and he close behind, Marta looked over her shoulder at me with disdain. "I knew the moment I laid eyes on you that you were no good. You came here to spy on the girls, eh? You're a dirty little fellow. I'd like to call the constables, so they could throw you in jail with the other criminals."

"I'm a musician," I said, pulling the two halves of my dress together to cover my exposed parts. "I respected the girls' modesty."

"How dare you speak to me of respect."

In the lobby, Carmine was at his post now. Silently he watched us pass. He looked wide awake, and nervous.

When we reached the landing outside the dormitory, Luca left me alone with Signora Marta for a moment.

"Signora, I must speak with you," I said. "You don't know what's going on here."

This only infuriated her more. "I don't know? Even now, you're ready to invent more lies. Say another word and I will call the constables. Just do as I tell you: go to your bed in the dormitory, get some other clothes, and come back here at once. And don't make a sound. Speak to no one. You have one minute. Disobey me and you go into the street naked."

I did as she ordered, first placing my clarinet and my few possessions and two soldi that I'd saved into my bag. I removed my torn dress and put on the one I wore to my audition, and then my cloak over that.

As I made my way back to the door in the darkness, one of the girls intercepted me. My heart skipped, for I hoped it was Adriana. But it was Prudenza.

"What's happened?" she whispered.

"I don't have time to tell you. You'll find out soon enough. I'm leaving the Ospedale."

"What?"

"Listen, Prudenza. You're all in danger here, especially Adriana. Warn her for me. Tell her I went to the wine cellar, pretending to be her, and exposed Aldo for what he is."

"I don't understand."

"He abuses girls, and blackmails them—and maybe arranges for them to be kidnapped. I fear that's what happened to Julietta. Signora Marta won't listen to me. Promise me you'll tell her what I just told you, even if she becomes angry with you."

Prudenza was frightened.

"Promise me," I repeated.

"I promise. But why are you leaving, Nicolà?"

I kissed her cheek and put my lips to her ear, "Because I'm a boy," I whispered. "Tell Adriana that, too," I added, without waiting for a reply.

In the corridor, Marta's anger seemed to have intensified greatly in the short time I was away. She looked me up and down, and I was sure she was going to slap me again. "How could you do this?" she sputtered. "You violated a trust."

 80

"I—"

"I don't want to hear your excuses." She yanked off my cloak. "Where do you think you're going with this? It doesn't belong to you."

"But it's freezing outside."

"That's your problem. You'll have to deceive someone else to get what you want."

Luca rejoined us, and they led me down the main staircase. I was heartbroken. Being expelled like this—my worst fear—I regretted even more that I had not revealed myself to Adriana before taking the chance I did. Now she'll find out I'm a boy, I thought, and never forgive me for deceiving her along with everyone else. It had been necessary for me to lie to Luca and Marta, but until that moment the true consequences of lying to my newfound friends hadn't fully hit me. They, too, would view me as an impostor.

We reached the lobby, and Carmine was not at his post. Luca called his name in vain, then went to look for him. Marta unlocked the front door and pushed me out into the night.

"Don't ever come back," she said. "We've never had such a scandal."

Suddenly I got up my courage. "You have a worse scandal than this on your hands," I said, and for an instant, before she slammed the door after me, I saw the surprise in her eyes.

My days as Nicolà Vitale were over. For better or worse, I was Nicolò Zen again.

8

I was shivering in the icy wind. My dress was so thin that I felt naked. I needed clothes—pants, a coat, whatever I could lay my hands on. From a cloudless sky the moon beamed down on the Grand Canal. The Riva degli Schiavoni was unusually empty, a few revellers on the footbridge, two priests boarding a traghetto, and a night watchman outside the money changers' arcade who eyed me suspiciously.

Clutching my bag, I turned up the alley beside the Ospedale. The high wall there was streaked with salt, from the sea winds. I passed through an iron gate with noisy hinges. Just beyond it, there was a blue door in the wall, which opened a few inches as I walked by.

"Psst," someone said. "Come here."

The kitchen's courtyard had two doors: one onto the garden, and this one. It opened wider as I approached, and Bartolomeo Cattaglia stepped out, holding a lantern. He raised it, lighting up my face, peering with his one eye.

"Nicolà? I thought it was you. My god, where are your clothes?"

I shook my head.

"Your teeth are chattering. Come in."

I felt ashamed in front of him, a man whom my father would

have respected. I respected him, too, and if I went in, I would have to tell him what a liar I was.

"Come," he said, putting his arm around me, and his wooden leg clicked on the stone tiles.

He had a fire going that warmed the entire kitchen. The evening cooking smells—onions, garlic sausages, broiled eel—still hung in the air. On the table a candle was burning beside an open ledger and a goblet of wine. Bartolomeo took a blanket from a bench and draped it around me.

"Sit down, please," he said. "Are you hungry?"

"No, sir."

"Would you like some tea?"

I nodded and he put a kettle on the fire.

"How did you know I was in the alley?" I said.

"I was doing my bookkeeping when I heard a commotion in the lobby. It was Luca and Marta arguing. Then Carmine joined in. I couldn't make out what they were saying, but it's unusual to hear people in the Ospedale shouting at this hour—or any hour. Moments later, I heard the gate open. And there you were." He eyed me closely. "But why were you there, Nicolà?"

I tried to revert to my natural voice, which was not easy at first. "First, sir, you had better call me Nicolò."

"Oh?"

I nodded glumly.

"I see," he said with a small smile. "You know, I suspected as much."

"You did?"

"Remember when I threw you the apricot?"

"Yes, I knew I made a mistake, catching it like that."

"It wasn't that you caught it with one hand. Don't deceive yourself: many of the girls here, dexterous as they are, could do the same. Or even that you dived. It was that you dived so recklessly, risking injury to your hands—and your good looks. Any girl who relied on her hands, and valued her looks, would have been more careful."

I couldn't argue with that.

"In fact, that merely confirmed my earlier suspicions," he went on. "You have neither the mouth nor the hips of a girl."

"Hips?"

"Yes. You don't swing yours at all. Every girl has a little swing to her hips. But you walk on the balls of your feet with your hips locked—like a boy. Anyway, all of this is beside the point." He sat down across from me and leaned his arms on the table. "I want to know what brought you to the Ospedale, what led you to attempt such a deception, and, especially, what just happened to you."

I told him my story, beginning in Mazzorbo and concluding with my expulsion from the Ospedale, emphasizing what had happened after Julietta's disappearance. I neither embellished nor suppressed any facts. Bartolomeo had seen plenty in his time, so I can't say he was surprised by any of it—I doubt much would surprise him—until I came to the events of that night.

He heard me out, shaking his head every so often, and after a brief silence said, "I understand your masquerade. You had lost your home and family, you were hungry and homeless. I tip my hat to you for knowing how to survive. As for the wine cellar, I'm disgusted with what you've told me, especially the presence of that stranger. I've known for some time that Aldo is no good. But

84

I didn't realize he was thoroughly rotten. At any rate, he could not have managed the activities you describe without assistance."

"You mean some of the girls?" I said, thinking of Marina and Genevieve.

"Perhaps. But he would require more substantial support than that."

"Luca?"

"Or Marta. I would wager it is one of them. If Carmine is involved, it is as their tool, no more. This is a nasty business. I need to poke around a little and then bring the matter to Master Vivaldi. He will listen to me."

"I'm sure that's true, sir, but no one is going to believe anything I say."

"I believe you," Bartolomeo said. "And the Master will, too. He and I have a good relationship. I once saved his life, you know."

"You did?"

"Five years ago. It was the sort of situation I had encountered around the waterfronts of a dozen ports, from Palermo to Xanía. Two toughs set upon the Master on the Calle Fondana. I happened to be passing. I thrashed one with my stick and sent the other packing. The Master gives me a case of wine every Christmas, and sometimes he comes here and we sit down for a drink. He trusts me." He chuckled. "It's a pity: if you were a girl, I would plead with him to reinstate you."

"A part of me is disappointed. The Master promoted me to Prima Clarinetto today. But I'll never have the chance to perform. A bigger part of me is glad I'm myself again. It will be good to put on a shirt and trousers. And not to be on guard all the time, covering my tracks. As I made friends, I hated having to deceive them, too."

"Friends like Adriana."

"Yes. I got tired of being a girl. Especially with her."

He smiled. "I understand. Still, to be named Primo—excuse me, Prima—Clarinetto. And to have the Master adapt his music for you. What a compliment. You must be damn good. And there must surely be another way for you to perform, outside the Ospedale."

"On the street?"

"No, no, professionally. If Vivaldi thinks you're that good, it means something."

I shrugged. "I hope so."

"Your time here had to come to an end eventually. I'm sorry it happened like this. But I'm glad to make your acquaintance anew, Nicolò Zen."

He extended his hand and we shook.

"You're still shivering," he said. "You need three things the way I see it: above all, some proper clothes; a place to sleep; and some money." He shook his head. "It's disgraceful that they kicked you out without a coat or a single zecchetto."

"I have two soldi I saved," I said, reaching into my bag.

He took a small box down from a shelf, opened it, and handed me some coins. "Now you have twenty," he said. "That's the easiest thing to take care of. Now, my quarters are too small—I'm used to it from living on ships—but you can sleep here, on the bench, and in the morning go to my sister's. She's a good woman, and she has a proper house in Santa Croce. She's a widow, and

 86

her two sons, my nephews, are in the Navy, deployed off Sicily. I know she will put you up until you figure out what you'll do next."

"Thank you, but I'd rather leave the Ospedale tonight. I don't want to make trouble for you."

"Ha. You think I'm afraid of Luca and Marta?"

"No. I would just feel better being away from here. It's asking a lot, but could I go to your sister's now?"

"It's not asking so much. I'll take you. And tomorrow you can go out and buy some clothes." He grunted. "Since you managed to get fitted for a dress, I'm sure you can find a coat and trousers. That leaves one item, which is clothes for you to wear until tomorrow. I'll be right back. Pour yourself some more tea."

After what I had been through, his kindness made me want to cry. But he was a war hero, a no-nonsense man who was treating me like a man—not someone I wanted to break down in front of. I simply wanted to thank him properly, and to add him to the list of people—that is, Signora Capelli, who rescued me on Mazzorbo, and Signora Gramani, the dressmaker—who had helped me when I was most vulnerable and whom I hoped someday to repay for their generosity. That day felt very far off; my prospects seemed even bleaker than the night I arrived in Venice.

Bartolomeo returned with a pair of canvas pants, a fisherman's sweater, and a short woolen coat.

"They belong to the gardener's son. You can borrow them for a day."

"Won't he miss them?"

"No. His father works for me, and he didn't object."

It took us twenty minutes on the empty streets to reach his

sister's house. I was impressed how quickly Bartolomeo could walk on one good leg. His sister was as he had described her: a stout woman with curly red hair and blue eyes who remained cheerful even after being awakened at two in the morning. He spoke to her alone for a few minutes and then rejoined me at the door while she made up a bed for me in her sons' room.

"How can I thank you?" I said as Bartolomeo shook my hand.

"You just did. I only wish I could do more for you."

III
Massimo Magnifico

1

"You have never heard of Massimo the Magnificent?" the woman said. "Are you not a Venetian?"

A swarthy, gray-haired woman with cold eyes and a clackety voice, she was the landlady of the late Signor Agnetti, the glovemaker who had given my father the clarinet that, to date, had brought me both good and bad luck. Agnetti had been one of six tenants who rented an apartment in the brown building the woman owned on the Calle del Forno, a sleepy side street in the Giudecca. We were standing outside her door beneath a low sky. A storm was approaching from the east. The first flakes of snow were falling.

"I am from Mazzorbo," I said.

"That explains it. I thought only geese and woodcocks lived there. And mosquitoes," she added with a smirk.

I didn't like this woman, but I held my tongue.

"Massimo is the greatest magician in Venice, maybe all of Europe," she went on. "I saw him myself at the Teatro dei Miracoli. Agnetti, may he rest in peace, was Massimo's cousin. They could not have been less alike. Massimo performs for kings and queens; Agnetti was a shopkeeper. He had no wife, no children, and no friends I ever saw."

"When did he die?" I said.

"Last November. He was three months behind in his rent.

His shop had been shuttered. He was skin and bones, coughing through the night. Keeping his neighbors awake. The day he died, I had gone to the constable to obtain an eviction notice." She shrugged. "Instead, they took away his body and confiscated what possessions he had left. He and Massimo did not get along. How could they have?" she added contemptuously.

I realized with some excitement that this Massimo was the cousin my father had told me about, who had given Agnetti my clarinet. It made sense that such an extraordinary instrument could be traced back to a magician.

"May I ask you where Massimo lives, signora?"

"Not many people know. But I do. My cousin's husband is an undertaker in San Polo. His place of business is across the street from a cobbler who is said to be Massimo's gatekeeper. Only the cobbler can provide outsiders with access to the magician's house."

"On what street can I find this cobbler?"

She curled her lip, which seemed to be her way of smiling. "That you'll have to find out for yourself. I've given you enough information."

I saw there was no point in pressing her further.

"Who are you, anyway," she said, narrowing her eyes, "and why are you so interested in Agnetti?"

"My father knew him. I wanted to meet him."

"I can't imagine why," she said, and with that turned her back on me and entered her house.

I couldn't have imagined, either, before Signora Botello, Bartolomeo's sister, put the idea in my head. With her sons gone, I believe she was happy to have a boy under her roof. Giving me a note for the owner, she sent me to the shop where she used to purchase her sons' clothes, and I was soon outfitted with a top-coat, trousers, three shirts, boots, and a felt hat. At my request, she cropped my hair short; my days of wearing it long enough to suit either sex were over. In fact, when she was half done, I asked her to cut off another couple of inches, so that it barely flared out from the sides of my hat. On my second night at her house, Signora Botello cooked me a fine meal of fried mullets and rice, and afterward asked me about my ill-fated tenure at the Ospedale. She did not condemn me for posing as a girl; in fact, she told me I should be proud I nearly got away with my ruse.

"And you were promoted to Prima Clarinetto!" she said with delight.

But when I told her the story of Aldo and the wine cellar, her mood darkened. "Don't worry about your friends," she said. "Bartolomeo will do all he can."

As it turned out, he did more than I expected. Several hours after Bartolomeo met with the Master, Aldo was expelled from the Ospedale. The Master was furious with Aldo, as much for his actions as the fact that he refused to divulge who his confederates might be. The Master forbade him ever to set foot in the Ospedale again. But because Aldo was blind, and ostensibly helpless in the world, the Master secured him a place in the boys' orphanage of San Benedicto at the eastern end of the Castello, near an iron foundry where many of the boys were sent to work. The orphanage was one of those stark, dark establishments I had dreaded. For Aldo it was surely an infernal transition: after having had the run of the Ospedale, his own room, and the powers—much abused—of a minor functionary, he was now one of two hundred members of a rough-and-tumble population in gloomy wards, a newcomer with no status or protection. Still, I did not underestimate his ability to overcome such obstacles, ruthless and amoral as he was. And when I thought of Adriana and Julietta, any sympathy I might have had for him evaporated.

Luca and Marta evidently informed the Master that I had run away. They claimed to be baffled as to why, and they did not inform him of my true identity, which surely would have cost them their jobs. When Bartolomeo met with the Master, he did not disclose my secret—which he knew could only further damage my reputation—but managed to implicate Aldo without mentioning my own visit to the wine cellar. The fact that Aldo had refrained from telling the Master my true identity, and thus getting Luca and Marta in trouble, convinced Bartolomeo that Aldo must be in cahoots with one or both of them. Aldo either feared retribution from them or hoped to serve them again.

Puffing his pipe at his sister's table, Bartolomeo said, "When the Master asked me if your disappearance could be connected to Aldo's corruption, I lied and said no. As for your friend Julietta, I haven't been able to find out anything. But I believe that Adriana and the other girls are safe for now. After what's happened, Luca and Marta won't dare to stir things up again."

After dinner, Signora Botello asked if I would play the clarinet for her. After all she'd done for me, I was happy to oblige her. She and Bartolomeo listened to me run through a portion of the Master's Sonata no. 6. I enjoyed playing for the two of them in that warm, quiet room. When I was finished, I saw the surprise in their faces.

"My god," Signora Botello said, "no wonder Signor Vivaldi made you a soloist. You could perform at San Angelo, or anywhere else."

"She's right," Bartolomeo agreed. "You do not need to be at the Ospedale to put your gift to use. There are many orchestras and chamber groups that would welcome you."

"You really think so?"

"I'm positive. Vivaldi heard it immediately. You said he told you so at your audition. Let me think about this."

This was the reason I sought out Signor Agnetti the following day: to discover anything I could about my clarinet, especially the origin of its powers and their true nature. If I was going to pursue the sort of career Bartolomeo suggested—which, I confess, felt like a wild fantasy—I needed to know if I could rely on my clarinet. With Agnetti gone, and the source of the clarinet revealed, I had an even better chance of acquiring this information.

I took a traghetto across the canal from the Giudecca to the Zattere and then followed the increasingly dense, zigzagging alleys into San Polo. By then, the snow was falling fast, disappearing into the canals and concealing the cobblestones beneath a shimmering carpet.

It took me two hours to find four funeral parlors, and none had a cobbler across the street. I thought my chances were better this way because I was sure there would be more cobblers than morticians in San Polo. I was wrong. Exasperated and cold, despite my new coat and boots, when I asked two porters carrying a table across the Campo San Boldo where I could find a cobbler, they directed me to an address, not five minutes' distance, on the

Calle Filosi. The cobbler's name was Gamba, and I was delighted to see that his shop was directly across the street from a mortician's parlor.

Signor Gamba was a thin, bespectacled man with rough, outsized hands and a shiny bald head. Neatly hammering nails into the soles of a blue shoe, he paused to allow me to introduce myself.

"I was told," I went on, "that you could direct me to the address of Massimo the Magnificent."

He looked me up and down. "Who told you that?"

"The former landlady of Signor Massimo's cousin, Benito Agnetti."

"And how would she know anything about it?"

"She said a relative of hers is the mortician across the street."

"Gandolfo?"

"I suppose so, sir. She didn't mention his name."

He thought about this. "And why would you want to see Massimo?"

This was the question I was waiting for. I took my clarinet out from inside my coat. "Massimo gave this clarinet to his cousin, who gave it to my father, who gave it to me. I need to ask him about it."

"It was Massimo's clarinet?"

"I believe so."

"Wait here," he said, putting down his hammer and disappearing through a curtain, into the back of the shop.

A moment later, he returned with a boy half my age who barely glanced at me before running out the door and down the street.

Gamba pointed to a worn bench behind me. "Sit there and keep silent," he said, and began hammering nails into the soles of the other shoe.

After about twenty minutes the boy returned, breathless, nodded to Gamba, and went back through the curtain.

"Come here," Gamba said. "I'm going to give you these directions only once, so pay attention. First, put on these blue shoes—they will fit you perfectly."

"But my boots—"

"Put them in this bag and carry them with you. And don't interrupt me again."

I hesitated, then pulled off my boots and slipped on the shoes. They had white soles. They seemed weightless. And they did fit perfectly.

The cobbler gave me directions. "When you arrive," he concluded, "give this to the footman." He handed me a small medallion embossed with a lightning bolt on one side and a closed eyelid on the other. "And do not remove those shoes until you are told to."

2

The address to which the cobbler directed me was in a courtyard off the Ramo Regina, a dead-end alley overlooking the Rio di San Cassiano, an unusually blue, almost turquoise, canal that connected the Grand Canal and the Rio della Madonnetta. I knew this courtyard was not far from the cobbler's shop, yet it took me an inordinate amount of time to reach it. I followed streets and alleys that, once entered, seemed to extend themselves with each step I took. The more I hurried my pace, the longer the streets grew. In fact, after turning off the Calle della Chiesa, putting the cobbler's shop behind me, I had the strange sensation that these streets and everything on them—houses, shops, even the pedestrians I encountered, faceless in the falling snow—had materialized only seconds before I appeared. As if none of it was any more permanent than the thick mist rising off the canal. The snow stung my cheeks, and I felt light-headed, with a cold pit in my stomach. Thinking it might offer me relief, I was tempted to take off the blue shoes and put on my boots. But I remembered the cobbler's warning. Venice is a labyrinth, where citizens as well as visitors can lose their way; but I seemed to have entered a more complex maze within the larger maze—at the center of the city, yet apart from it, so murky it was as if I were wandering inside someone else's dream.

Finally I was so dizzy that I stopped and leaned against a

wall and closed my eyes. I counted to twenty, to calm myself, but when I opened my eyes again, I became even more disoriented: no longer leaning against the wall, I found myself at my destination, a courtyard at the end of the Ramo Regina. There were four small houses on the ramo, then the courtyard, surrounded by a high wall with an iron gate. On a brass plaque beside the gate was the street number the cobbler had given me. Only one thing was missing: the house to which the courtyard should have been attached!

I could see the leveled rectangular plot where a house ought to stand, and the bushes that would have flanked it, and even the outline for a path from the courtyard to the front door. But no house. There was only a small park on the far side of the courtyard. At its center, there was a marble bench and a white statue. As I walked across the courtyard, I saw that the statue was a tall, mustached, long-haired man in a cape and boots. He was standing atop a lion and a leopard, one foot on each, brandishing a sword. His blank eyes were turned to the sky. There were statues of lions all around Venice, for it was the symbol of the city, but I had never seen one like this. I circled the statue twice before sitting down on the bench. The afternoon had flown by. Dusk was coming on, and though the snow was falling harder than ever, the gray clouds parted suddenly for a ray of orange light that turned the Rio di San Cassiano into molten lava and the brick walls and paving stones of the ramo into bars of gold. Everything became so bright that I had to cover my eyes, and it was only then, through the chinks between my fingers, that I saw the house to which the park and courtyard belonged.

It was a large white house, four stories with a white-tiled roof and tall windows with white shutters. In fact, every aspect of the house—doors, chimneys, cornices, metal fixtures—was white, including the limestone path to the front door.

The house must have been there all the time, I thought with a shiver, invisible to me until that orange light appeared. Yet as the clouds closed up again, and the light faded, the house remained, and the amber lamps on either side of the door began to glow.

I gathered my courage and walked to the door. The door knocker was a white lightning bolt. A footman answered my knock. Short and bald, he had a flat, impassive face. His hands and feet were no bigger than a child's. His face was pale and his irises black, as if they were one with his pupils. He wore an ivory earring in his left ear and was dressed in white from head to foot.

"Coat," he said.

I removed my clarinet from the inside pocket before he took my coat and hung it in a closet.

Then he held out his hand, palm up. I had forgotten about the medallion. I dug it from my pocket, and before he closed his fingers on it, I could have sworn the eye on the medallion was now open.

He pointed toward a long hallway and said, "Inside."

He led me down the hallway, around a corner, and through a low archway. We were in a small white room, containing only a white carpet and table on which there was a vase of white flowers. This room, in turn, led to a slightly larger room, with a larger table, carpet, and vase, on and on, through a series of Moorish archways, five rooms in all, each a purer white than the last, so that by the fifth room the table and carpet were barely distinguishable. In that room, too, I discovered that the carpet was comprised, not of wool, but hundreds of butterflies that every few seconds fluttered up to the ceiling and returned to the floor in unison. And I realized there were other creatures present, an owl that swooped by and a lizard skittering into the corners, they, too, so white that they were only visible, three-dimensional, for an instant before literally disappearing into the woodwork. I could barely discern the footman anymore, until he stopped and turned around in the last archway, even his pale face standing out against that whiteness. He beckoned me into an enormous, four-storied room filled with marvels even more spectacular than the butterfly carpets.

On platforms hung by wire from the ceiling beams there were white trees on which doves were perched, singing, preening, darting between branches. The ceiling itself was glass, but the snow falling outside was passing right through it, dissolving before it reached the floor. In the center of the room three marble mermaids stood atop a circular fountain, poised to dive into the milky water. Incense was burning in braziers. There was a pyramid of birch logs in the fireplace, ready to burn. And everywhere I looked, elaborate stage props: silver hoops, birdcages, swords and daggers, ropes, nets, chains, a small mountain of trunks and boxes, and the only colored objects in sight, relegated to a half-hidden alcove: a set of frightful masks and two red and green Chinese cabinets adorned with dragons and tigers. I was trying to absorb all of this when I came on a succession of wall mirrors that reflected me as I passed—that is, some image of me that did not belong to my body or wear my clothes, but instead was white and transparent, like a ghost. I froze before the last of these mirrors, my heart pounding so loudly that the footman had to shout to get my attention.

"Sit," he repeated.

I took the chair he indicated, clutching my clarinet. I understood now why it had been fashioned of the whitest ivory, rather than wood.

"Wait," the footman said before disappearing through a low door.

It was clear he only spoke one word at a time, out of choice or necessity I didn't know. But there were more compelling mysteries to occupy me in the minutes I spent alone in that room, gazing at the birds and watching the snow fall, and, after hearing a splash, turning to find one of the mermaids missing. If all of this is an illusion, I thought, the magician who created it must be unimaginably powerful, and as if on cue, a booming voice echoed from behind me.

"Good evening. Didn't Lodovico offer you tea?"

To my astonishment, the speaker was the man depicted in the statue outside, tall and imposing, with the long hair and mustache, which were jet black. In fact, except for his face, everything about him was black: velvet robe, silk pants, leather gloves, boots. He was powerfully built, with broad shoulders and large, nimble hands. His huge eyebrows, like streaks of black paint, converged over his nose and curved back to his temples.

"Lodovico!" he shouted, and the footman appeared from the low door. "Bring the boy burdock tea, with a plate of figs and jam." He looked at me. "Would you care for anything else, Nicolò?"

"No, thank you, sir." I saw that his eyes had immediately gone to my clarinet.

"Call me Massimo. And come, warm yourself by the fire."

What fire? I thought, until I realized the birch logs had started burning on their own.

I sat on an ottoman near the fireplace, and Massimo in a high-backed chair whose arms were carved into serpents. Seated, he somehow appeared even taller, looking down on me. His gaze was intense, but I tried to meet it, and not shy away. Lodovico brought me my tea and figs. Inhaling the vapor off the tea, I wondered what burdock was.

"It's a medicinal root," Massimo said. "Drink this tea every day with honey and you will strengthen your mind. Try it."

I took a sip. Even with the honey, it tasted bitter.

"Before we go any further," Massimo said, "I would like to hear how you acquired the clarinet."

Though this was my reason for being there, I hesitated. The landlady had made it clear that Massimo wasn't fond of his cousin; I was wary that the story around my clarinet, and Signor Agnetti's role in it, might somehow offend Massimo and incur his wrath.

"Don't be afraid. Just tell me."

I did so, and he listened closely. Nothing seemed to surprise him, but he did betray a faint smile when I mentioned my brief stint with the orchestra at the Ospedale.

"So Signor Vivaldi made you Prima Clarinetto. Would you play me something?"

I froze. I hadn't expected this, and with his eyes upon me, I wasn't sure I could concentrate.

"Play anything you like," he said.

I put the embouchure to my lips, closed my eyes, and launched into one of the solos I had played with the orchestra. The sound carried well in that room, and when I finished, Massimo nodded approvingly.

"Excellent. I am so pleased to find the instrument in such deserving hands."

"Thank you, sir."

"Only a man like my cousin would never have tried to play this clarinet," he said with a frown. "I made him a gift of it, and he thought it could only be valuable because it is ivory. I told him it had more significant qualities, but I knew he wasn't listening because he only measured value in karats—and this clarinet is very light, is it not? He had no imagination. And he was a terrible businessman, always just a step ahead of the debt collectors. At any rate, after your father chose the clarinet—fortuitously for you—my cousin would have comforted himself by calculating the value of the ivory in relation to the labor your father rendered him and deciding he had gotten the better of the deal." Massimo chuckled. "If this were a typical clarinet, of ebony or rosewood, or even the elephant tusk from which it was carved, that might have been the case. But it is not, as you discovered within moments of receiving it. No doubt you have a wonderful ear, and a real talent, but would you like to know how you came to play so beautifully, so quickly, an instrument you had never laid eyes on?"

"Very much so."

"I assume you had never even heard of the clarinet."

"No, sir. Even the Master had little knowledge of it."

"Is that so," he said, clearly pleased to hear this. "I acquired this one in Leipzig, from a famous instrument maker, on my last tour of Germany. It was the ivory that attracted me. I was assured it was one of a kind. Then I learned what a unique instrument

 104

the clarinet is, so new to the world. I felt I could make this one even more unique, so when I arrived home, that's what I did." He paused. "Do you know what a spell is? Forget about the tricks of hypnotists and witches. A true spell is rooted in chemistry and physics, not trickery. All things are composed of particles, and all particles are composed of atoms, which are invisible, even through a microscope. If one can rearrange those particles, and rechannel the energy that animates them, he can make an object—or even a living thing—behave differently. Everything is changeable because atoms are constantly in flux. A fallen leaf decays into soil, a fish is eaten by another fish, stones and shells break down into sand. All of nature is governed by laws. But if someone has the focus and concentration to bend even one of those laws, he can alter its connection to all the others. Do you understand, Nicolò?"

"I think so." I understood about the soil and the sand.

"Imagine pulling a single thread from a fabric, which then unravels." He pointed to the ceiling. "Or altering the composition of a pane of glass by diverting the energy that binds its particles just enough to make it permeable, at a certain temperature, to flakes of snow. Or rearranging the components of a musical instrument so that the energy a musician brings to it produces the notes he hears in his head. It is not just an extension of him: it is one with him."

I nodded. "Yes, that's how it is when I play the clarinet."

He smiled. "I know. I put a spell on this instrument that would enable the very first person who attempted to play it to forge this connection and make music with extraordinary skill. Man or woman, old or young, that person, and only that person, would be able to play the clarinet flawlessly from the first, so long as he could harness his concentration and energy. My cousin could read music, and because our relationship was so strained, I hoped the clarinet might bring some joy into his life. I should have known he wouldn't try to play it, and clearly your father didn't before he presented it to you. You were the intended one. And your friend the cook is correct: now the clarinet can give you an entirely new life as a performer."

"And my ability to play it—"

"Will remain as it is. The clarinet is yours. And only I can reverse the spell on it."

"Thank you, sir."

"It is my pleasure. There is only one condition: you must never give or sell the clarinet to anyone, under any conditions."

"I would never do that."

"Should you no longer want it, you must return it to me. Keep it close. If you allow it to be stolen, even if you are not directly at fault, I will hold you responsible." He stood up. "And you don't want that to happen."

I shook my head.

"Good. Many people owe me favors, Nicolò. One is a music impresario named Emmerich Hoyer. He books engagements for some of the finest musicians in Europe. I am going to give you a letter for him that will ensure that he helps you in any way he can. But you must set out to see him without delay, as soon as you leave this house. When you do, your fortune will be made."

"In what part of the city will I find him?"

"He is not in Venice. You will be leaving Venice."

"When?"

"At once. Can you do that?"

"Tonight? Can I say goodbye first to Signora Botello and Bartolomeo?"

"I'm sorry, but no."

"They have been so kind to me."

"I will inform them, I promise you."

"My clothes—"

"Lodovico will pack a bag for you, with clothing and provisions. It will be a considerable journey."

"Where am I going?"

"Vienna."

"Austria?"

"It is freezing at this time of year, but also quite beautiful. Most importantly, there are musical events every night—operas, concerts, recitals. Herr Hoyer will find you living quarters and see to your other needs. Are you ready to do this?"

I was overwhelmed. I didn't fully grasp the implications of what he was proposing—how could I?—but I followed my instincts. "I'm ready," I replied.

"Come with me, then."

I followed him down a long hallway, parallel to the one by which I had entered with Lodovico, but deeper inside the house and even more private. We passed several curtained windows, and then one that overlooked the Rio di San Cassiano. Massimo stopped and beckoned me to his side. Night had fallen. The canal shone in the darkness beneath whirling snowflakes. A lantern bobbed on the quay where a constable was making his rounds.

Massimo did not say a word. He lifted one finger and pointed it toward the canal, and in a burst of light that blinded me momentarily, the water was replaced by a forest of sunlit leafy trees that stretched all the way to the Grand Canal.

I gasped.

"What is your favorite fruit?" Massimo asked calmly.

"I—"

"Quick."

"Oranges."

Before the word left my lips, there were clusters of oranges hanging from all the trees. Where the constable had walked there was a farmer with a basket picking the fruit.

"Now close your eyes and count to five," Massimo said, "then open them again."

When I did, the trees were gone, and the snow was sifting into the dark canal.

"How did you do that?" I said.

He shook his head. "Never ask how."

He led me to the end of the hallway, where a door opened onto a library with floor-to-ceiling bookshelves, a rack of rolled-up maps, and several globes and astrolabes. There was a telescope at the window and a microscope on a table beside a tray of glass jars filled with powders, unguents, plants, and insects. Only four candles were burning, so the room was not nearly as bright as the rest of the house.

"Wait here while I write you that letter," Massimo said, entering the adjoining study and closing the door.

Gazing around at the thousands of books bound in white leather, I discovered I was not alone. There was a girl in the cor-

 108

ner with her back to me taking a large book off the shelf. She was wearing a white dress and white slippers, and her long hair was tied back with a white ribbon. She turned around and walked toward me, and I was stunned to see that it was Julietta.

"Julietta!"

She shook her head and smiled. "That is not my name."

Indeed, she did not speak in Julietta's voice.

"Julietta della Tiorbo," I said, "from the Ospedale della Pietà."

She laughed. "Della Tiorbo—is that a real name?"

"Then you must be her sister, or her cousin. She is from Verona."

"I have no sister, and I am Venetian, not Veronese."

"Who are you, then?"

"Massimo's assistant, of course." She was standing beside me now. She opened the book and handed it to me. "These are his chronicles. You think the orange trees were something? Look at this."

Across the two pages of the open book were a series of color drawings, beautifully detailed. Frame by frame, they depicted Massimo onstage performing one of his signature acts: a box containing a mouse expands and contains a cat, expands again and contains a dog, then a baby, then a horse, and finally an elephant; at which point Massimo directs the audience's attention to the uppermost balcony of the theater, where his female assistant, flanked by the cat and the dog, is cradling the baby.

"That is the act that made him famous," the girl said. "He first performed it in Parma, for the Duke."

"The assistant—is that you?"

"Does it look like me?" she smiled. She turned several pages, to another color drawing. "This was before the King of Poland, at his court. Massimo conjured an entire forest in the great ballroom. All around the audience, up and down the aisles, there were trees. Birds filled their branches and wind rustled their leaves. The taller ones swayed. Someone shouted out that trees were cropping up around the castle, into the surrounding streets, across Warsaw, until suddenly Massimo clapped his hands and it all disappeared. I was there with him that night." She closed the book and patted the cover. "There are many such wonders in these pages. Nearly everything he has ever done."

She walked back to the bookshelves and replaced the book. Massimo came out of the study and handed me an envelope.

"Time to go," he said.

As I followed him from the library, I glanced back at the girl and stopped short. "Adriana," I murmured, for now she looked exactly like her.

"Come, Nicolò," Massimo said, pulling me into the hallway.

"How does she do that?" I said.

"She can resemble whoever you might have in your mind at that moment."

"She can read my thoughts?"

"Not exactly. Think of it this way: you project an image and she reflects it, like a mirror. Before an audience of five hundred, she will appear to be five hundred different girls, but only one visible to each member of the audience. Her name is Meta. You'll meet her again."

Before I could ask any more questions, we were in the foyer, where Lodovico was waiting with a leather rucksack. My boots had been placed before a chair, on which I sat and removed the blue shoes. There was a long, narrow window beside the door, and I glimpsed the small park with the statuary. The lion and leopard were clearly visible, but the statue of Massimo was gone. I was certain of it. A moment later, Lodovico brought me the rucksack and planted himself before the window, blocking my view.

As I pulled on my boots, Massimo said, "At the entrance to the ramo, turn left and follow the Calle della Rosa to the Grand Canal. A boat awaits you there at the dock. It will carry you across the Lagoon to San Giuliana. There you will find the coach in which you will make the rest of your journey. The bag contains all you need except these." He handed me forty soldi. "Keep them on your person until you reach Vienna."

"Why are you doing all this for me, sir?"

He brought his large hands together. "Never ask how, and never ask why. But this one time I will answer you. I, too, was orphaned as a boy. I was completely alone, with no resources. A Turkish magician, Hajik Nassim, rescued me from the streets. I already had a gift for magic, and he became my mentor. I owe everything to him. Music is your gift, Nicolò. Fate put this clarinet into your hands. You can accomplish glorious things with it. Don't let the opportunity pass. I look forward to seeing you perform on a great stage and receive the accolades you deserve." He extended his hand. "Until then, good luck."

3

After I stepped outside and pulled my hat down against the howling wind, I saw that the statue of Massimo was back in the park, but without any snow sticking to it, though several inches had collected on the backs of the lion and the leopard. Could the statue really have left the park? Could it be Massimo himself, in the guise of marble, brandishing the sword? Having just witnessed some of his feats, I was not prepared to dismiss such a fantastical question. I hurried my pace, and at the gate glanced back once more, half expecting to find that Massimo's house was no longer visible. But it was there, all right, the windows bright and smoke curling from the chimneys.

The route to the canal was as clear and direct as Massimo had indicated. The maze I had stumbled into earlier was gone. The streets were deserted. Sheets of snow blew off the rooftops. The powder crunched under my boots. On the grounds of the Palazzo Moro two hounds were baying. Across the canal the Palazzo Fontana was pitch-black. I found a sleek caorlina awaiting me at the dock. It was manned by two oarsmen in black slickers and hoods. I settled into my seat, and without a word they started rowing, making good speed in the choppy water. Freezing spray blew into our faces, blinding me, but the oarsmen never faltered. The Grand Canal was also unnaturally empty: we passed a single gondola and a s'ciopò, a shallow fishing boat with an old man at the tiller, hugging the shore. Leaving the canal for open water, I felt a wave of fear and apprehension. I had never sailed across the Lagoon in this direction, never set foot on the mainland. My longest journey had been from Mazzorbo to Venice. Now I was going to a place about which I knew nothing, where I had not a single acquaintance and could not speak a word of the language. As for Venice, I could not bear to look back at its lights, knowing that the Ospedale's must be among them, that at this hour Adriana would be preparing for bed, and Signora Botello would be setting out dinner, and Bartolomeo, who was to have joined us, would be worrying about me.

The farther we sailed, the rougher the water and fiercer the wind. I was afraid we might capsize, but the caorlina was resilient and the oarsmen expert. Though it took nearly an hour, we came ashore finally at the small fishing village of San Giuliana. One oarsman remained in the caorlina while the second led me up a wooden ladder to the pier. We walked around the shuttered customs house, to an inn called the Marbella. Two drunken men were arguing at the entrance. Their voices sounded as if they came from the bottom of a well. Beside the inn, by a trough, there was a black coach drawn by four white horses. Two men in black slickers and hoods sat atop the coach. On its doors the letter M bisected by a lightning bolt was painted in white. The oarsman opened one of the doors, and I had barely clambered in when the coachman cracked his whip and the coach lurched forward.

We headed north to Mestre at a rapid clip. The road was rough and slippery. Riding in a carriage was another first for me. And what a grand carriage it was. There were two wide seats, cushioned in velvet, on which four people could easily travel in comfort. For someone my size, all alone, it felt enormous. The curtained windows could be sealed with sliding panels of glass. Brass candleholders were set into the leather walls. There were woolen blankets and sheepskins and pillows, each embroidered with an M. Long drawers beneath the seats contained bottles of wine and jars of dried fruits and nuts. A third drawer, off to the side, was locked. There was a jug of drinking water. And a cabinet filled with books, playing cards, dice, and a chessboard.

I opened the rucksack and saw that Lodovico had indeed been thorough. There were two crisp white shirts, a pair of black pants, socks, and a striped vest. For victuals: two loaves of bread, a round of Asiago cheese, olives, a jar of jam, preserved figs, a bag of burdock root tea, and salt cod. Suddenly I was hungry, and I ate some of the bread and cheese with figs.

The coach rattled and its wheels whined as we passed through Mestre and turned onto an even rougher road to Mogliano Veneto. From there, for three days and nights I rode alone through valleys and over mountains, in and out of a succession of towns and villages: Preganziol, Treviso, Oderzo, Aviano, Cavasso Nuovo, Tolmezzo, Dogna. Their names sounded beautiful to me, like a long musical progression. I stayed in inns where Massimo's name, which the coachmen gave the innkeepers, secured me a hot supper and a warm, airy room with a feather mattress. Staying in an inn—a far cry from the rundown boardinghouse where I lived before entering the Ospedale—was as wondrously strange to me as riding in a coach. But more exciting was the realization that these were the very first times in my life I had a bedroom to myself. Lying in the darkness, gazing at the starry sky through the window, listening to the muffled sounds of men drinking and

 114

talking in the tavern below, and then the deep silence that settled over the entire establishment when the other guests were in bed, I was surprised to find that I did not feel lonely. I was comfortable being alone in those rooms, and that was something that would serve me well in the coming months.

On the morning of the fourth day, the fifteenth of February 1715, we reached the frontier at Tarvisio and crossed into Austria on a narrow mountain road. It was a brilliantly clear, cold day, and my enduring memory is of the towering pine forest we rode through and the powerful scent of the trees and their blue needles flashing with ice. After a night in Villach, where the food was suddenly Austrian—pork sausages, cabbages, and red potatoes—we proceeded north by northwest to Vienna.

I would not set foot in the Venetian Republic again for nearly two years.

IV
The Prodigy on Tour

1

Less than a month after my arrival in Vienna, I played my debut recital to a full house at the Kundstaafe Theater on the Hafenstrasse. Accompanied by a harpsichord and a violin, I performed four sonatas composed by Domenico Scarlatti and the Trio in D major that Arcangelo Corelli composed for the Queen of Sweden. Emmerich Hoyer, my manager, had encouraged me to explore Corelli's music, which was familiar to me, as well as Telemann's and Handel's, which was less so. He gave me lessons in etiquette and advice on how to deal with the varieties of people with whom I would be mingling. Over supper at his club, he introduced me to businessmen who were his friends, and more importantly, to some of the elite Austrian musicians he represented. Herr Hoyer opened up many doors for me in Vienna, where he moved with ease in high society and intellectual circles. Due to his efforts, the Kundstaafe was filled with an expectant crowd that evening. Hoyer had spread the word in the newspapers, salons, and coffee shops of the city that a young Venetian, a prodigy hailing from the only European city that could rival Vienna musically, would make his international debut. Sotto voce he hinted that I had been personally mentored by Antonio Vivaldi, which of course was a gross exaggeration. Because Hoyer had an impeccable reputation for promoting talented musicians, he was able, in a very short time, to lay down the foundation of my own reputation, which until the eleventh of March 1715 had been nonexistent. After that performance, and three others in rapid succession in April, I was indeed deemed a prodigy by the powers that be—critics, royal patrons, even local composers—and Hoyer had to turn down more engagements than he could accept. He billed me as "Europe's first clarinet soloist," which, though it made me cringe, was in fact true. But when I took my bows after those first performances, I never forgot that my true mentor was Massimo the Magnificent, and that while my father's prophecy had been correct—*You will go into the world and gain fame and fortune*—my mother's comment about my skill on the clarinet was closer to the mark: *It's a miracle.*

Emmerich Hoyer was a short, stout man of fifty, with a florid complexion and blond hair that seemed to be standing on end at all times, defying gravity and weather, rising from his head like a plume. He had an identical twin named Heinrich, the police commissioner of Vienna, whose blond hair also stood on end. Once at a reception at the opera house, and another time leaving a coffeehouse, I mistook Heinrich for Emmerich, greeting him warmly and receiving a stony look in return. Trained as a lawyer, Heinrich had the soul of a policeman. I felt reflexively guilty in his presence—for what crimes, exactly, I couldn't say. Without any basis in fact, I feared that Heinrich, of all people, who knew nothing about music, rather than Emmerich, who knew everything, would somehow discover the secret of my clarinet. For while Emmerich was critically, passionately perceptive, which was his business, Heinrich was coldly, scientifically suspicious, which was his.

Emmerich Hoyer wore well-tailored, expensive suits, silk

shirts, a red cloak lined with ermine, and a collection of broad-brimmed, brightly colored hats. Fortunately for me, his Italian was as good as his German, and from the moment I arrived at his large house on the Friedrichstrasse, he rarely stood on ceremony and was patient to a fault. When I discovered how impatient he was in his dealings with others, including his employees, his browbeaten wife, Carole, and diffident son, Wilhelm, recently expelled from the university, I wondered why he treated me, a nobody, so well. I didn't delude myself that it was because of my personal charm, or even my musical talent, though he had been mightily impressed, even enthusiastic, when I played for him after he had read Massimo's letter with obvious skepticism. Any doubts he had, I put to rest. But he was accustomed to dealing with talented musicians: that was his business, and it didn't always entail his exuding warmth or even friendliness with clients. No, I was convinced that he was especially attentive to me because he feared Massimo and wanted to please him. It turned out that was true, but also more complicated than I could have imagined.

Hoyer found me a furnished flat on the Braunerstrasse, just off the Albertinaplatz, only a few blocks from his own home. It consisted of three high-ceilinged rooms and a balcony—impressive in itself, but overwhelming to a homeless Venetian boy—on the fourth floor of a large white building with a marble stairway.

"I would have you live in my house, my boy, but trust me, with the career before you, you will want your own place. Anyway, this is what Massimo requested. Twice a day I will have one of my housemaids, Gertrude, come here to clean and cook for you. She is an excellent cook. She worked for Albinoni when he lived in Vienna, and became adept at preparing Venetian dishes."

He seemed especially pleased to inform me of this. I thanked him for securing the apartment so swiftly, and the food with which he had stocked the kitchen, and the clothes he had had me fitted for at his tailor, including a formal black suit for the performances I would give.

"It must have cost a lot of money," I added, taking in the gleaming oak floors and the ornate mantelpiece.

"It's nothing," Hoyer said with a dismissive wave. "The receipts from your first recital will pay for all of this, and more. My office will draw on your account with us to pay your bills. I am in and out of Vienna these days, so when you need cash, or anything else, you should inform my assistant, Stefan, or Otto, the book-keeper."

Gertrude, a spry young woman with very blue eyes and perfect teeth, refused to speak to me until I first addressed her. I asked her to dispense with this formality—later on, when I was settled in, I even ordered her to—but she wouldn't relent. In the morning she had hot chocolate and rolls on the table as soon as I was up and around. At dinner, she prepared whatever I had requested earlier in the day. (Her grilled eels with onions and currants, Venetian style, really were excellent.) She also brewed a cup of Massimo's burdock tea for me every night. I practiced on the clarinet every afternoon for five hours. They were my happiest hours of the day. My exploration of the latest compositions that passed through Hoyer's office, from my distinguished fellow Venetians, Antonio Lotti and the brothers Marcello (Benedetto my favorite), to the greatest Austrian composer of the day, George Frideric Handel, who was producing masterpieces with frightening ease, to a pair of famous French composers who had recently visited Vienna,

Jean-Philippe Rameau and François Couperin. No matter how much I was abetted by my clarinet, practicing difficult compositions of this quality honed my concentration and helped me to absorb the music more deeply, interpret it more intensely, and carry its beauty inside me. Nothing had ever comforted me like music—not when I was a boy without prospects in Mazzorbo or now, when I was being groomed to be a topflight performer.

I often told Gertrude to forget her cleaning chores and instead sit and listen when I practiced. This was not because I needed an audience to feed my vanity, but rather because I felt uncomfortable about having a servant—treating someone born into my own social class, if not higher, as if I were her superior. I told myself it wasn't an imposition to have Gertrude listen because I knew that, like so many Viennese, she loved music. And wasn't it better for her to listen to music than scrub the kitchen that much more? The trouble was, she was so diligent that she ended up doing both. And she was so well trained, and proud of her training, that she would only go so far when I attempted to treat her as an equal; when I asked her to join me at the table for dinner, or even hot chocolate, she categorically refused.

I found a nearby coffeehouse that I frequented, and a restaurant where I ate lunch so often that, after I'd made a name for myself, the maître d' held a corner table for me. Mostly I walked around the city, stunned by the size of the plazas, the public parks, the broad boulevards, the enormous ornate fountains with their cherubs and nymphs. Venice is a small city; its complexity makes it feel large. But one can walk from one end to the other in a couple of hours, at most. Vienna seemed to me to have no perimeters. I could feel the vastness of Europe stretching out in all directions. Since it was the only other capital I had ever been in, I assumed that other cities that were still just names to me—Paris, Berlin, Prague—must be equally large, if not larger. And noisy! The vessels on Venetian canals are relatively silent. One will hear the flapping of a sail or the plash of an oar or the creak of a rudder, but Venice has no carriages or wagons, and the only horses, outside of the Lido, where the rich can canter along the sand, are workhorses at the loading docks in Santa Croce. As a Venetian, I was accustomed to walking, and despite its great distances, I usually made my way around Vienna on foot.

I had heard from Hoyer, and then seen for myself, all the damage inflicted on the city in the recent past. Like Naples, and Venice in my grandfather's day, Vienna had been hit hard by the plague. Beginning in 1680, the epidemic came in waves, killing thousands of people, emptying entire villages in the outlying countryside. For twenty years, whole neighborhoods were abandoned, overrun by vermin, destroyed by the elements. What the plague spared, the Turks destroyed when the Ottoman army laid siege to the city, lobbing mortars and firing cannonballs over the fortifications. Gradually the Turks were beaten back, never to return, and by the time I arrived in the city, the last breakout of the plague had ended and the rebuilding of the city was under way. In fact, there was a burst of new, large-scale building, much of it originating in the blueprints of Italian architects hired at great cost.

Exploring the city nearly every afternoon, I inevitably gravitated to these construction sites. There was the enormous Belvedere Palace, built for Prince Eugene of Savoy, the hero of the Turkish Wars, who was universally hailed as the savior of Vienna.

And the Palais Kinsky, its stone blindingly white in the midday sun. And, most poignant for me, the great Karlskirche Cathedral on the Karlsplatz, commissioned by the Emperor Karl VI two years earlier. I often stood for hours at the edge of the work site, watching the stonecutters, carpenters, and masons on the high scaffolds and thinking of my father. The men were so small against the blue sky, kneeling or stretching on the narrow planks, chiseling limestone and laying mortar. The icy wind was blowing right through my heavy woolen coat and gloves, and I imagined how numb those men's hands must be, how heavy their tools felt, how much colder and swifter the wind must be three hundred feet off the ground. I said a silent prayer that none of these men would fall as my father had, and through all the days the Karlskirche rose up before my eyes, no man did.

In late afternoon I liked to visit the long park that wound along the western bank of the Danube. Having always lived on the water, I sometimes felt trapped, spending most of my time at the center of a landlocked city. Wide as the Giudecca Canal, choppy and green, with screaming terns circling overhead, the Danube made me feel at home. In the hour before sunset, I liked to sit on a bench by the riding trail and watch the Danube turn deep blue. Barges from Germany and Romania sailed by, and fishing boats casting their nets for bass and sturgeon. Couples pulled up in carriages and strolled under the trees. On the opposite bank, flocks of geese pecked at the grass.

On a day that Gertrude informed me was the coldest in years, I saw blocks of ice floating down the Danube, refracting the light like huge diamonds. It had been snowing for two days, and men in white coats were shoveling the main streets. At dusk I started walking home. I stopped to buy cheese and apples from a stall in the Kohlmarkt. I walked up the four flights to my flat and unlocked the door. Gertrude must have just left: birch logs were burning in the fireplace and a casserole of sausages and potatoes was on the table. I hung my wet coat by the fire. Though the room wasn't dark, it felt so, and I lit more candles. Then I cut a thick slice from the loaf of freshly baked bread and sat down to eat. Only after I had bathed and put on my robe, and settled before the fire to practice for another hour on my clarinet, did I open the plain brown package Gertrude had left for me on the coffee table.

Though I had insisted to her that I could barely read German, she was convinced that anyone who could play music as I did must know the language of Vienna. She had picked up enough Italian to get by from Albinoni and the numerous Italian musicians who visited him, but I told her that if she really wanted to help me learn German, she must speak it to me at all times, pointing to objects and using sign language, if necessary. She accommodated me in this. Inside the package was an Italian-German lexicon that Stefan, at Hoyer's office, had obtained for me. I had quickly learned the German for "clarinet," *die Klarinette*, and "prodigy," *das Wunderkind*. I learned the phrases that enabled me to order a meal or ask for basic directions on the street. But late one night I realized that there were words I wanted to know for myself, in German as well as Italian, even if I never used them with anyone else. *Einsam*, for example, and *verloren*, and *heimwehkrank*. The first two, "lonely" and "lost," should not have been surprising; but I hadn't expected to seek out the third word, "homesick." I honestly didn't think I could feel homesick when I no longer had

 126

a home, or at least a home of the kind I had known, however humble. This was doubly confusing when, at the same time, I now had a home all my own, which was highly unusual for a boy my age, Austrian or Venetian. The word in Italian was more beautiful, *nostalgico*, but when I woke alone in the middle of the night, *heimwehkrank* sounded more the way I felt.

3

What was it like to become a celebrated soloist in Vienna? Terrifying, thrilling, beyond anything I had imagined, much less experienced. At first it all seemed to be happening to someone else. The huge audiences; the stage that floated in the darkness like a ship, with me and a few other musicians on deck; the deference paid me by some of those musicians after they first heard me; the envy I felt from others; the ovations and encores; the glittering receptions; the postconcert banquets of lobster, caviar, sturgeon, and wild boar hosted by Vienna's most affluent residents, bankers and barons who could not have guessed they were fêting a boy from the rough, remote island of Mazzorbo, where the finest holiday menu consisted of broiled eel and cornmeal and a salad of dandelion greens.

I performed with quintets and trios, with the Royal Orchestra at the Imperial Opera House before twelve hundred people, before the Archduke's brother at the Hofburg Palace. I revelled in it; it was a transcendent time for me, playing fabulous music with the finest musicians. My repertoire kept expanding, fed by the vast amounts of Austrian and German music I encountered: Bach and Froberger, Kerll and Pachelbel, as well as Italians I had never heard of like Carissimi and Poglietti. When there was no clarinet part in the score, as was often the case, I assumed the musical line assigned to the flute or trumpet, playing the high and low octaves accordingly. The sheer volume of performances Hoyer booked for me, and the quality of the musicians with whom I played, enabled me to hone my technique and achieve the subtlest effects. My interpretive skills increased tenfold. And my ability to concentrate for long stretches, shutting out the rest of the world, ensured that my clarinet never failed me. Not once.

Hoyer leased me a well-appointed coach and sent me on tour, occasionally joining me in the cities near Vienna. I performed in Linz, Pressburg, Salzburg, and Munich, as far north as Stuttgart and as far west as Zurich. Hoyer's assistant, Stefan, a gangly young man who dressed like a deacon, was my constant companion. He kept to himself, a man of few words and fastidious habits: polishing his boots every night, trimming his beard every other day, praying aloud before every meal. Our routine seldom varied. On travel days, we rode through deep forests and vast fields of wheat and corn. Spectacular vistas opened up before us: snow-capped mountains and silver alpine lakes and enormous billowing clouds, just above the peaks and therefore closer to the earth than they would be anywhere else. We passed other coaches, lone horsemen, farmers with ox-drawn carts, and occasional platoons of Austrian soldiers as well as Bavarian stragglers making their way across the Tyrol. When we arrived in a city, we checked into one of the best hotels. I bathed and changed my clothes. Stefan attended mass at the nearest church. In the afternoon we went to the concert hall so I could rehearse with the local chamber group or orchestra with whom I would be performing. We returned to the hotel, where I dined early and took a nap. Then we went back to the concert hall for the performance. Invariably there was a reception afterward hosted by local dignitaries. Then to bed. Stefan's job was fourfold: keep me on schedule; see to my needs; deal with the local promoters and managers; keep track of receipts and transfer funds to Vienna.

Everything proceeded without incident until we arrived in Ulm and I got drunk for the first time in my life, on white Rhine wine. I had played eight concerts in ten days and was exhausted. It was a hot August night. We were in a hotel on a small lake. We ate on the terrace, and after dinner Stefan went up to his room and I stayed outside, listening to the crickets and gazing out over the water. The surface was silver beneath a full moon. If I closed my eyelids halfway, I could have been in Venice, in Burano maybe or at the tip of the Lido. As was his custom, Stefan had drunk two glasses of wine. Before the waiter could take away the bottle when he cleared the table, I poured myself a glass and drank it down like water. It was sweet. I drank another glass, and my stomach grew warm and my head light. All my weariness from performing and traveling seemed to seep away. I asked the waiter for another bottle and some fruit, as I had seen Hoyer do at the end of every meal. Two more glasses of wine and I found myself on the shore of the lake, weeping. I was thinking of my mother and father, of my sisters, of Julietta and Prudenza, and most of all, of Adriana. I feared I would never see her again. Never be able to explain to her what had happened during my last night at the Ospedale. I had refrained from sending her a letter, knowing Marta would intercept it, which would only make things worse for Adriana. I would have given anything to see her, knowing that if she inquired about my whereabouts from Bartolomeo, he would tell her that I had simply disappeared without a word of farewell—or thanks. No matter how persuasively Massimo reassured him, the fact remained that I had disappeared a second time, and I was certain she would think even less of me for it.

My thoughts went round and round like this—I don't know for how long—until I felt someone patting my cheeks and sprinkling water on them. I opened my eyes and wondered why I was looking straight up at Stefan and the waiter and why they loomed so large over me. I realized I was lying flat on my back on the coarse soil with the bottle, nearly empty, planted beside me. They helped me up and Stefan dismissed the waiter. He put his arm around me and guided me toward the hotel. As we climbed the grassy slope, I pushed him away, bent over, and threw up. It took me a minute to get everything out, and the next thing I remembered, it was morning and I was lying on top of the bedclothes wearing my shirt and pants.

Fortunately I didn't have to perform that night. My head was splitting. But riding to Stuttgart on a pitted road was no respite. When we arrived, I was hungry but had no desire to eat. I couldn't rid myself of the taste of the sausages I had consumed the previous night, in fact every night since leaving Vienna. I was sick of every kind of sausage the Germans made, and their hard black bread, and their diced potatoes swimming in butter. I missed Gertrude's cooking, but even more, I craved the simple spicy food enjoyed by even the poorest Venetians: grilled fish and pasta, olives and peppers. For the rest of my tour, I abstained from sausages, and ate mostly bread, cheese, and pickles. And I didn't drink again for a while. Stefan kept a closer eye on me, and stopped ordering wine with dinner, which was certainly unnecessary. As we were returning to Vienna by way of Innsbruck, he informed me that Herr Hoyer was going to be extremely pleased: in addition to being so well received, my performances had garnered receipts of forty-two thousand marks.

"Which means, Nicolò, that after Herr Hoyer takes his commission and deducts expenses, you yourself will be depositing roughly twenty-eight thousand marks in the bank. Congratulations."

Until then, I had never deposited or withdrawn a single pfennig or zecchetto at a bank. In fact, aside from the morning I visited the Banco del Giro with Herr Hoyer to open an account, I had never even set foot in a bank.

Though I now had firsthand experience of fine hotels, expensive restaurants, and the best tailors, the amount of money Stefan mentioned, and the fact it was mine, was beyond my comprehension. As it turned out, those sums amounted to only three-quarters of what I actually earned; the other quarter Stefan had systematically concealed and attempted to steal from Herr Hoyer and me by partially diverting the transfers intended for Hoyer's bank in Vienna to his own bank in Pressburg. I was sorry to learn that Stefan was so dishonest, and such a pious hypocrite to boot, but not nearly as sorry as he was when Herr Hoyer discovered his treachery, and—even worse for Stefan—when Massimo learned of it.

 132

3

I learned how to hold a girl in my arms and kiss her in a lavish apartment on the Kaplanstrasse, a boulevard lined with poplars trimmed to the exact same height. I remember the details of the place clearly: a line of tall windows with sky-blue curtains, birch logs sprinkled with frankincense crackling in the fireplace, the strong perfume of lilies wafting up from a lush garden. There was also a vase of those lilies, freshly cut, on the drawing room table. Above the mantelpiece there were assorted paintings of horses: grazing beside the Danube, carrying cavalrymen into battle, racing around a track. The dining room was entirely walled in mirrors and illuminated by purple candles. A portrait of the dowager Empress in her youth dressed up as Pallas Athena—armor, scepter, plumed helmet—hung beside the door. The marble sinks had gold fixtures. In the parlor there was a plush divan with golden pillows. The parquet floor was inlaid with suns and moons composed of quartz. I had never seen such things before, and imagined that only men like the Doge or the Pope could possess them. However, far more memorable and precious to me was the first kiss I received from Madeleine Pellier, the younger sister of the Marquise de Montal, on that divan. Estranged wife of the Marquis, the Marquise was a vivacious young woman of twenty-two. Her name was Noémi. She was quite beautiful; men could not take their eyes off her. Seven years younger, her sister Madeleine shared her good looks. In fact, because the resemblance between them was so strong, and because the Marquise looked younger than her years while Madeleine looked older, people often mistook them for one another. But they were very different: while Noémi (after our first meeting, she told me to stop calling her Marquise) could be moody and secretive, given to long silences, Madeleine was spontaneous and open, with a sweet, clear voice and infectious laugh.

The sisters had come to one of my performances at the Kärntnertor theater. I was playing an all-Poglietti program with a string quintet. At the reception afterward at the Aldenfer Hotel, I was introduced to her by an old friend of Hoyer's, Baroness Mannheim, a statuesque woman of forty whose husband was the commissioner of public works. The Marquise was sitting at a corner table sipping pink champagne when the Baroness led me over to her. She was wearing a deep blue gown. She had a full figure, intense brown eyes, and honey-colored hair that framed her face. Her features reminded me of the famous statue of Minerva in the Metzenplatz, but softer. She was the sort of woman men fell in love with at first sight. For a boy of fifteen, she seemed unattainable, as indeed she was. But I sensed that the same could not be said of Madeleine, who joined us a few minutes later. It was not just her easy demeanor, but in fact the way she looked at me as she sat down beside her sister and announced in a crisp, clear voice, "You were just splendid tonight, Herr Zen. We must talk all about it."

She was the image of her sister, all right, but slenderer, with slightly darker, longer hair, a less pronounced Gallic nose, and blue eyes rather than brown. Their lives were inextricably linked:

 134

orphaned young, they had lived with their grandmother, a genteel woman in failing health who spent the last twenty years of her life as a kind of shadow. To save herself and her sister from poverty, Noémi had set out to find a husband. With her good looks and former lineage, she didn't have to search for long. At nineteen, she married the Marquis de Montal, a man Madeleine detested and Noémi herself did not particularly like. It turned out to be an even bigger mistake than either of them had imagined. Quickly, unhappily, Noémi discovered that the Marquis, a quick-tempered, taciturn man more than twice her age, had a greater passion for gambling and prostitutes than for her. During his initial infatuation, he had been on his best behavior, impressing her with his wealth and his powerful connections at Court. He had wined and dined her in Lyon and given her expensive jewelry. He had been solicitous of Madeleine, showering her with gifts as well and promising to become her guardian and protector. The daughters of a minor official with thwarted ambitions, the sisters were susceptible to the Marquis's overtures. He and Noémi were married in the chapel on his estate in Quercy. Madeleine was the maid of honor. Three hundred people attended.

Five months later, the Marquis abruptly announced that he was bored with the Marquise and was setting out for Marseilles and Nice on business; that is, the business of frequenting casinos and brothels. He expected his new wife to remain on the estate, overseeing the household and maintaining appearances. He slashed her personal allowance and cut off Madeleine's completely. Realizing he had shown his true character, Noémi did not attempt to dissuade or even reproach him. She bided her time until the day he left, then told Madeleine to pack as many of her things as she could carry, took her own jewelry and all the money she could lay her hands on, opened a line of credit at the Bank de Lyon, and ran away, first to Paris, then Vienna. She didn't know if he would come after her; so far, she had only received two letters, forwarded from Paris: an angry one from her husband himself and a threatening one from his lawyer. Meanwhile, she had enough money so that she and Madeleine could live extravagantly for some time, in Vienna or any other city. She apparently wasn't thinking too far into the future, but Noémi did know this much: she had made many friends among the nobility in both Paris and Vienna, none of whom doubted that, if the Marquis were to divorce her, she would quickly make a new match. The fact she had fled her husband, and was fast acquiring a reputation for wildness, seemed to make her all the more desirable. And the younger version of her that was Madeleine even more so.

The Baroness left us alone, and when two army officers immediately came over and engaged Noémi in conversation, Madeleine took my hand and led me to a table on the veranda, signaling a waiter for more champagne.

She began speaking to me in French, but checked herself when I shook my head.

"Italian?" she asked.

"That would be better."

"My sister says you are a genius, Nicolò Zen. Your music is heavenly. So tell me about yourself."

I wasn't just flattered, I was smitten. By now, I had met a good number of beautiful women and girls in society, but always formally, alongside their husbands or parents, as you would expect. Many of the married women had sons and daughters older than me, and the girls my own age had been in sophisticated company all their lives. I had never had any of these girls approach me so boldly, with so little pretense and so much warmth, taking me aside as if she wanted me all to herself. Which, in fact, she did. Just a few months earlier, I could not have imagined such a scenario. I drew on the poise I had developed onstage and the reserve Hoyer had advised me to maintain when I was in society, speaking little and cultivating what he called an aura of mystery. I was still too green to be starstruck around famous people, but Hoyer liked to remind me that during and after my performances I was the star. Yet to these affluent people, I was also an oddity, because of my class as well as my age. Many of them looked on me warily. As members of the gentry, they were accustomed to being admired, and I—a boy many rungs down the social ladder—was putting them in the position of admirers. In Mazzorbo, where everyone but a few landowners was poor, I felt far removed from issues of class. Struggling to get by, we lived every day with the consequences of class, but with little time to ponder its workings in that larger world which remained unreachable and abstract for me until I arrived at the Ospedale and learned some hard lessons. In Vienna, rubbing elbows with princes and ministers of state, I was continuing my education. Lesson one being: however precocious my talents, I was there to entertain, they to be entertained, and when I was gone, someone would take my place. Perhaps I would be remembered, even venerated, as Hoyer insisted. He truly believed in me, and promoted me relentlessly, helping me to achieve great fame in a short time. I really was considered the first true solo clarinetist in Europe, a groundbreaker, just as Massimo had predicted. My performances were analyzed and acclaimed. I was indulged, celebrated, fêted. My reputation began to outpace my comprehension of it. Composers were inserting clarinet parts into their scores, not just in Vienna, but in Venice and Paris. Hoyer told me that Vivaldi himself had featured prominent clarinet solos in his newest opera, *Juditha triumphans*, which premiered in Padua. It amazed me that I might have inspired the Master.

How much had all this gone to my head? Enough so that when a girl of Madeleine's class approached me, I was excited, momentarily flustered, but not completely surprised. I had heard that Viennese girls in high society were precocious and flirtatious; past the age of sixteen, they enjoyed a good deal of latitude in their relationships. Evidently this applied to girls visiting the city as well.

Madeleine Pellier wanted to know about me, but what on earth was I going to tell her?

She made it easy for me. She began with an observation. "Do you see that gray-haired lady sitting with the young officer? That's the Baroness Manzer with her lover. She is forty-five years old and he is twenty-seven. In France that would be unusual, even scandalous. Here it is the norm. Older women are respected for their experience. And girls are expected to become experienced sooner rather than later. It's very civilized, even by French standards, don't you agree?"

How could I not, especially the way my pulse was racing.

Madeleine shrugged. "I have not been in Vienna long enough to know. My sister keeps a tighter rein on me than she ever has on herself. When it comes to men, she's a bit of a hypocrite in more ways than one. But enough of that. What about you, Nicolò Zen?

In addition to your talent, you're a very handsome fellow. And you're a Venetian. Have you had many lovers?"

I had only a few seconds to decide whether to tell the truth. When I opened my mouth to reply, Madeleine smiled.

Leaning closer to me, she reached across the table and took my hand. "Wouldn't you like to escort me home?"

I glanced over at her sister, still chatting with the two officers, who were fawning over her.

"Oh, she'll go out to supper with one of them—or maybe both," Madeleine said wryly. "She'll let me take the carriage."

Ten minutes later, we were crossing the Josefsplatz Bridge in the Marquise's gilt-trimmed coach.

"Are you hungry?" Madeleine asked. "We have a wonderful cook."

Indeed they did. A light supper of cheese and meat was laid out for us in the dining room, and the maid who served us uncorked a bottle of champagne. I barely touched my food, and after my experience in Ulm, made sure only to drink one glass of champagne. When Madeleine took my hand and led me back down the hall to the parlor, I felt lightheaded, as if I had drunk the entire bottle. When we passed the master bedroom, I noted that the maid had turned down the sheets and coverlet on the large bed and lit only two candles, which glowed amber in the darkness. Yet another vase of lilies filled the room with its perfume. A bottle of brandy and a pair of crystal goblets sat on a silver tray on the bedside table.

"As you can see," Madeleine said archly, "Noémi will be home tonight, but not for a while."

In the parlor, new logs had been placed upon the fire. The curtains had been discreetly drawn. Madeleine led me directly to the divan, nestled close to me, and put her lips to mine. She did it again, her eyes twinkling as she inclined her head and this time applied more pressure and ran her tongue along my lips. I parted them, and her tongue met mine and slowly twirled around it. I had never kissed, or been kissed, like this, and drinking in her perfume, feeling the warmth of her body against mine, I did what came naturally, and put my arms around her.

Pulling her close, I felt a tingling down my spine, and a warmth and well-being that seemed to suffuse every inch of me. I wanted to hold on to this moment as long as I could. I thought of the beautiful Venetian ladies I had seen on the quays as a boy— how remote, and untouchable, they seemed. But now, lost in our kisses and caresses, I couldn't imagine any of them being as beautiful as Madeleine.

Gradually my thoughts took a darker turn. The fact that Madeleine had marveled at my musical talents began to gnaw at me. I enjoyed being praised by professional musicians, and however alien it had been to me not so many months earlier, I had grown accustomed to receiving adulation from strangers; but after the short, delicious time we had spent together, Madeleine was no longer a stranger in my mind. As the very first girl I ever kissed, she never would be. But her praise reawakened the grave misgivings I'd had about fooling my friends at the Ospedale—about being an impostor. I was hungry then, just off the streets, and didn't have the luxury of following my conscience rather than my stomach. In Vienna I was anything but hungry, and my conscience was tugging at me. Increasingly there were moments onstage when

140

I could not rationalize how I had become so proficient on the clarinet. I told myself that it was my fingerwork, my breath, that brought the notes into the world, willing them into existence, but only after I had clearly, concretely imagined the sound. This took real skill and intuition, even on an enchanted instrument. Could I have played the way I did without Massimo's assistance? Not likely, but no longer impossible, I reassured myself, thanks to the arduous regimen I maintained, practicing for hundreds of hours and performing constantly. However, in order to retain my self-respect, I knew I had to test this proposition one day soon, taking the stage with another clarinet in hand, for example.

But that day had not yet come, I thought, as Madeleine sighed and laid her head on my shoulder. I was enjoying my taste of the good life and I didn't want anything to jeopardize it for a while.

We had just heard a coach pull up on the street below, and the sound of a woman's laughter, so we knew we only had a few more minutes together on that night.

"It's Noémi," Madeleine said simply, smoothing out her dress and standing up. "You had better go."

"Will I see you—?"

"Tomorrow, I hope. Will you join us for breakfast?"

"I would love to."

"Come at eleven o'clock." She smiled and kissed me once more, on the forehead. "Noémi likes to sleep late."

I didn't know how I could make the hours fly by fast enough, but I would try, I thought, as the Marquise breezed into the apartment moments before the maid showed me out.

"Herr Zen," the Marquise exclaimed cheerfully. "I hope Madeleine was a good hostess."

"Very good," I said. "Good night, Marquise."

"Please, call me Noémi. And may I call you Nicolò?"

"Of course." I made an awkward bow and headed for the stairs.

"He is adorable, Madeleine," I heard the Marquise say as the door closed behind her.

In my haste, I nearly bumped into a tall, uniformed man at the foot of the stairs. It was one of the officers who had joined the Marquise at the reception at the Aldenfer Hotel.

He was annoyed, but as soon as he recognized me, tipped his hat and said, "Excellent concert, young man. Welcome to Vienna."

4

I awoke at dawn, bathed and dressed, and when Gertrude arrived, told her I would not require breakfast. Accustomed to preparing me hearty meals in the morning, she must have been surprised by this information, as well as the fact that, formally dressed, I was vigorously polishing my best black boots. But she asked no questions.

At eleven o'clock sharp, I arrived at the Marquise's apartment. A different maid let me in, and while there was as yet no sign of the Marquise or Madeleine, a table in the parlor was laid out with a pot of steaming coffee, hot cinnamon rolls, raspberry crêpes, and a bowl of oranges.

The Marquise came into the room in a yellow silk robe. Her hair was perfectly combed, but she wore no makeup, and looked as if she had just emerged from sleep.

"Come, have an orange, Nicolò," she said by way of greeting. "They were a gift from Baron Stösser. He brought orange and lemon trees all the way from Sardinia, and he grows the fruit in his orangerie. His son Konrad brought them over for Madeleine and me."

At that moment, I was amazed to discover that, in addition to the pleasure I had derived from embracing and kissing Madeleine, and savoring her company, I had apparently, within hours, acquired an entirely new set of feelings that included jealousy.

Though for all I knew Madeleine and the baron's son were passing acquaintances, the mere mention of him as a fellow visitor got my imagination working, and I felt a pang in my chest. Until the previous night, I had never kissed or touched a girl as I had Madeleine, and suddenly I was brooding over whether I had rivals for her affection. In a matter of hours, my hubris had expanded far beyond the concert stage.

As the maid poured me coffee, Madeleine appeared, also in a silk robe, with red slippers to match, and flashed me a smile. She looked even more beautiful in the daylight. "I am so happy to see you," she said as I stood up to pull out her chair. I was grateful for Herr Hoyer's lessons in etiquette, which were already paying dividends.

Throughout breakfast, I could barely take my eyes off Madeleine, but the Marquise was far more engrossed by the series of notes delivered by the footman and handed to her by the maid than by the two of us, much less the rolls and crêpes.

Afterward, Madeleine saw me to the door, squeezed my hand, and kissed me on the lips.

"Come back tonight," she whispered, "when Noémi is out."

And I did.

V
Maximus Grandios

1

What made my liaison with Madeleine all the sweeter was that she behaved as if she couldn't get enough of me. Perhaps it was the novelty of my origins (I told her how I had been orphaned and made my way, omitting my stint at the Ospedale, of course); or the possibility that her passion for my musicianship (she attended all my performances) had spilled over into a physical attraction; or, best of all, that she simply found me irresistible. After two weeks in which I had visited her every night, I became so cocky and indiscreet—dressing to the nines and putting on cologne when I went out—that Gertrude felt compelled to step out of character long enough to give me a gentle warning.

"Do be careful, Herr Zen," she said, helping me on with my jacket. "You're a fine young gentleman, but remember: for anyone who becomes so famous so fast, the snares of the city are especially treacherous."

I thanked her for what I heard as a compliment, but was deaf to her advice. It was impossible for me to think of Madeleine as someone to avoid—not when I longed to be with her more— even when I reminded myself of the obvious: she was perhaps an even more temporary resident of Vienna—as she had hinted to me more than once—utterly dependent on her unreliable sister, a married woman on the run from her husband.

It took the unexpected appearance of that husband to bring

this home to me. He arrived in Vienna on the afternoon of August 25, the very day I would make a discovery that not only altered my relationship with Madeleine and diverted my musical career, but made me flee Vienna.

It was a summer day so hot that clouds of steam were rising from the many fountains along the Klappersteinstrasse. I had left the Marquise's apartment at noon after another leisurely breakfast with Madeleine, picked up some money at Hoyer's office, and was walking carefree toward the river, where I knew I would find a cool breeze. When I stopped beneath a shade tree to eat a chocolate given me by the Marquise's maid, Margot (who by that time had become complicitous in my nocturnal visits), I spotted a colorful poster on a nearby wall that stopped me cold:

WORLD-FAMOUS CONJURER,
NECROMANCER & PRESTIDIGITATOR
MAXIMUS GRANDIOS
PERFORMING IN A LIMITED ENGAGEMENT
AT THE TOFFENKLAUS THEATER
AUGUST 25–29, 8:00 O'CLOCK

I had learned enough German to know that *Grandios* meant "Magnificent." And that *Maximus* was the German for *Massimo*. My heart skipped a beat: was Massimo performing in Vienna? And, if so, why hadn't I heard about it before? I hurried to the Toffenklaus Theater, just a few blocks away, where I found a more detailed poster at the main entrance that baffled me even more. The conjurer depicted on the poster was not Massimo. He had close-cropped blond hair, blond mustache, blue eyes, pointier ears than Massimo, and a squarer, Germanic jaw. On his palm he balanced a miniature man in full evening dress. The man looked bewildered, as well he should, for this was supposedly one of Maximus Grandios's signature feats: taking a volunteer from the audience and shrinking him to the size of a mouse.

I bought a ticket for that evening's show and went directly home, where I found Gertrude preparing my lunch.

"Tell me, Gertrude, what do you know about a conjurer named Maximus Grandios?"

She answered almost exactly as Signor Agnetti's landlady had when I asked about Massimo the Magnificent. "Everyone in Vienna has heard of Maximus Grandios," she said. "The greatest magician in all of Austria."

"He lives here, in Vienna?"

"Of course."

"For how long?"

She looked puzzled. "As long as I can remember."

"Have you ever seen him perform?"

"Once. With my sister. But we left early."

"Why?"

"My sister grew frightened. She said his tricks did not seem like tricks. And that all magic is black magic." Gertrude paused. "She is very religious."

"But what frightened her?"

"When he made a man disappear—a silversmith—she was sure the man had really disappeared." She averted her eyes. "I thought it was a trick."

"Yet you haven't gone to see Maximus again."

"No." She wiped her hands on her apron. "I had a friend who knew that silversmith. About two weeks after Maximus's performance, I met her on the street and she told me the silver-smith had disappeared that same night. No one had seen or heard from him. People said he had run off with a woman, or was in trouble with the police."

"Were the police called in?"

"The chief of police was at the theater. He is a friend of Maximus's. He assumed the silversmith had fled the city for personal reasons."

"What was the trick Maximus performed?"

"The silversmith went onstage and Maximus's assistant gave him a pair of shoes to put on."

"What kind of shoes?"

"Ordinary-looking shoes. They may have been green—or blue. The silversmith put them on and stepped inside a circle of candles the assistant lit. From the shadows, Maximus asked the silversmith where he would most like to be if he could be any-where else in the world. The silversmith thought about it, and replied, 'India.' Maximus closed his eyes, clapped his hands, and the silversmith was gone without a trace. Like everyone else, I thought our eyes had deceived us and that he would reappear at any moment. When his seat remained empty, I figured he must be backstage. That's when my sister grew agitated. And she wasn't surprised two weeks later when I told her the silversmith hadn't been seen at his shop or his house. 'If he returned by sea,' she said, 'it would take him longer than that.'"

"And did he return?" I asked.

Gertrude shook her head. "No, Herr Zen. And I heard that Maximus has never performed the trick again—not in Vienna, anyway."

I was in an aisle seat in the second row when Maximus Grandios came onstage and bowed. He was dressed in white from head to toe. He was as tall and formidable as Massimo Magnifico, with a similar aura of confidence and power. At first glance, he didn't much resemble Massimo, but there were certain elements—sharply angled left eyebrow, thin upper lip, broad uncreased forehead—that, when looked at discretely, reminded me of Massimo. In fact, if I reassembled Maximus's face in my mind using only those elements and leaving the rest blank, I might imagine I was looking at Massimo. Because of that, and his name, of course, and his monochromatic costume, I knew I had to meet Maximus Grandios face to face.

The crowd was enthusiastic, buzzing in anticipation, leaping to their feet as one to applaud Maximus's entrance. It was clear that many of them had been drawn to the theater for something more than light entertainment. There was an edginess, a sense of danger, arising from the mere fact of their having entered Maximus's domain, where any one of them could meet the fate of the silversmith.

Maximus's props consisted of three curtained booths, a gold pyramid with a triangular door, and a cauldron dancing with flames. The backdrop was a scarlet curtain on which gold and silver birds were embroidered—except that they were moving, flitting from point to point, sometimes flying off to circle beneath the theater's domed ceiling before returning to the fabric of the curtain. All through Maximus's act, those birds were in motion, yet so intense was his presence, and so startling his conjurations, that they barely distracted me.

Without addressing the audience, Maximus began abruptly with a twist on the conjuration that had carried off the silversmith. Standing at center stage, he closed his eyes, pressed his fingertips together, and called out, "Now, Friedrich!"

A few moments later, a woman in the third row jumped up from her seat. "It can't be!" she screamed.

"Please stand, Friedrich," Maximus said calmly.

A middle-aged man in the seat beside the woman stood up and looked around apprehensively. He had long gray hair and stooped shoulders. His eyes were blank and his movements stilted. He was dressed in farmer's overalls, wearing a straw hat and mud-coated boots.

"Tell us where you came from," Maximus said to him.

"I-I—"

"But how did he get here?" the woman cried. "He hasn't been to Vienna in years."

"Please, madame," Maximus said, "bear with me. It's all right, Friedrich. You were at your farm, correct?"

The man nodded.

"And where is your farm located?"

The man cleared his throat. "Outside Pressburg. I just left the barn."

"And the lady beside you is your cousin, correct?"

"My cousin, Anna, yes. But who are you, and where are we?" he stammered.

"Anna," Maximus said, "is this your cousin Friedrich, from Pressburg?"

The woman was frozen now, speechless in her fright. Finally she nodded assent.

The audience, stunned into silence at first, burst into applause, after which they began talking excitedly among themselves, asking one another how this man could have materialized suddenly. "Yes, I swear, his seat was empty," I heard a man in the third row exclaim.

"Quiet!" Maximus boomed, and as soon as the audience settled down, he called out, "Come, Fiona."

A few seconds passed, and another audience member, an elderly man in a middle row, cried out in astonishment, "My god, it's her!"

Maximus went through the same gentle interrogation, establishing that the young woman in a blue coat was indeed Fiona, the daughter of the elderly man. She was a dressmaker who resided in Bottenheim. She was as disoriented as Friedrich from Pressburg, her eyes vacant and her hands shaking, but she embraced the elderly man, and said, "We're in a dream, Father. Don't be afraid."

Again the audience applauded wildly. Apparently Maximus Grandios could not only make people disappear; he could also make them *appear*, transported from distant places. And not just any people, but the kin of audience members.

With a lesser magician, one might conclude that these random audience members and appearers had been planted, but I didn't believe Maximus had done that. For this to be a hoax, all of them would have to be superb actors, with near perfect timing. No, whatever the underlying facts, I had just witnessed a conjuration of the first order, which only the most accomplished magician could pull off, as fantastical and inexplicable as anything in Massimo's repertoire.

After levitating a woman from the audience, and releasing seventeen doves from a basket that looked as if it could hold no more than two, Maximus delivered an aside about the number 17 in his rolling bass voice: "It is a number associated with water: on the seventeenth day of the second month, the Great Flood began; after his tryst with the nymph Calypso, the Greek hero Odysseus put to sea on a raft for seventeen days; and from its source in the Black Forest to its mouth at the Black Sea, our Danube River is seventeen hundred miles long." Moments later, he performed the feat depicted on his posters: a man six feet tall, in evening dress, stepped from that golden pyramid twirling a cane, walked into the first booth and reemerged three feet tall; entered the second booth and reemerged one foot in height; then went in and out of the third booth and ended up, six inches tall, with a toothpick for a cane, in the palm of Maximus's hand.

The audience greeted this feat with loud gasps and bursts of applause, but in a matter of seconds, I lost interest in it, and all that had preceded it, from the appearers to the levitating woman, when Maximus's assistant walked onstage for the first time.

I recognized her immediately: a slender, long-legged girl wearing a black silk dress and silver slippers. Her long hair was tied back with a black ribbon. A burning taper in each hand, she held her head high and moved gracefully. She seemed as supremely

 154

confident as Maximus himself. Slowly she scanned the audience without pausing to meet anyone's gaze—until she came to me. Our eyes locked, then she smiled and looked away.

It was Meta, Massimo's assistant! I was certain of it. My first impulse was to rush backstage the moment Maximus completed his curtain calls. But I checked myself. Yes, there was a remote possibility that this was the same girl I had met in Venice. Or, more likely, her Viennese counterpart, a conjurer's assistant with the same unique ability to reflect whatever image a member of the audience might project upon her ("like a mirror," as Massimo had said). Just as in Venice Meta had appeared to me to be, first Julietta, then Adriana, this girl could be appear to be Meta herself. Unnatural as it seemed, was it really that much of a jump to think I might be projecting onto this conjurer's assistant the image of the only other conjurer's assistant I had ever encountered?

My head was spinning with these questions as I watched Maximus and the girl part the scarlet curtain and disappear.

I could have ascertained Maximus's address the following day and attempted to pay him a proper visit. But I didn't want to wait that long. Stepping outside the theater, I put up my collar against the wind and rain. Hailing a cab, I instructed my driver to wait by the entrance to the alley that led to the stage door. I watched the audience stream from the theater, chattering about Maximus's act. Last to exit were Maximus's "appearers," without their various relations. Linking arms, they floated down the street and, like pale shadows, dissolved in the mist.

As I strained to see some trace of them, a silver coach drawn by four black horses thundered up the alley and sped around the corner. I glimpsed Maximus and the girl inside, peering out their windows. I ordered my driver to follow them, and we were off, up the Kohlstrasse, onto the Boulevard Hauser, around the green marble fountain in the Kirchnerplatz, and down a succession of narrow zigzag alleys. Maximus's coachman snapped his whip over the black horses, and I was fortunate to have a driver who, with two aging workhorses, managed to stay close behind. Our chase ended abruptly at the south end of the Kundenstrasse.

Set on a broad lawn behind an iron fence, Maximus's house was flanked by a windowless church and a substation of the metropolitan waterworks. It was an imposing residence, four stories of black granite, with a black-tiled roof and black shutters. The doors and chimneys, and even the path to the front door, were black. It was like a dark mirror image of Massimo's Venetian villa. But there was no park off the cobbled courtyard, and no imposing statue, just an enormous oak tree whose upper boughs were lined with dozens of crows, gleaming in the rain.

I watched Maximus and the girl step from their coach and enter the house. I waited a moment as their coach continued around the house to a stable, then paid my driver and walked up to the front door. The door knocker was a black lightning bolt.

The footman who opened the door was short and bald, but otherwise did not resemble Lodovico, Massimo's footman. He had a hatchet profile, long nose, and a short red beard. He wore a black patch over one eye. His livery was also black. Like Lodovico, he wore a single earring; but it was in his right ear not his left, and it was onyx to Lodovico's ivory. And unlike Lodovico, he spoke more than one syllable at a time.

"Come in," he said.

 156

"Thank you. And your name would be . . ."

"Ludwig. My master is expecting you."

Ludwig is the German version of *Lodovico*; that it was the footman's name did not surprise me as much as the fact that Maximus was expecting me.

"Let me dry your coat," Ludwig said. "Please wait here."

He carried away my coat and I gazed down three long hallways that emanated from the foyer. They were lined with pots of black flowers whose rich, peppery fragrance filled the air. I expected everything in the house to counterpoint the contents of Massimo's villa—black rooms, furniture, carpets—but it wasn't like that at all. The hallways were painted yellow, the doors blue, and the Turkish carpets a swirl of colors. The chandeliers' red crystals cast sparks off the ceilings. And the draperies depicted scenes out of Greek mythology—Atalanta and her golden apples, Hephaistos throwing his net over Ares and Aphrodite, Hades's abduction of Persephone—which I recognized from a book that Madeleine sometimes read aloud in bed. Actually, because my knowledge of French was scant, she would first read a passage, then translate it into Italian for me.

Ludwig returned and beckoned me to follow him down the middle hallway. The five doors off that hallway were shut. But as we approached the last one, it opened and two black mastiffs emerged and began circling me. Had they reared up on their hind legs, they would easily have been taller than me. But they were friendly, and after sniffing me closely, they retreated. Next I heard a loud tinkling, and a half dozen black cats wearing bells on their collars ran past us. At the end of this hallway, we entered a large circular room with a domed ceiling. An oak table sat at the center of the room beneath a massive candelabra. Though it could easily seat twenty guests, there were only three place settings at one end. The plates and goblets were silver and the napkins linen. On the lower third of the wall there was a three-hundred-sixty-degree mural of Chinese pilgrims disembarking from barges on a broad river and marching along a dusty yellow road, through forests and fields, over rocky hills, and up a steep, dangerous path to a mountaintop temple glittering with sunlight. The pilgrims numbered all varieties of humanity: princes and beggars, athletes and cripples, warriors and priests, nuns and courtesans, the old and the newborn. I felt that even if I gazed at it for days, or weeks, I would barely take in its details. But as incredible as the mural was, it was the floor in that circular room that riveted me. The octagonal tiles were not marble or stone, but glass, beneath which pale green water was flowing fast, punctuated by flashes of color—red, orange, yellow. They were fish!

"An underground tributary of the Danube flows beneath this house," the voice of Maximus boomed. "The ancient tribes that inhabited this valley took sustenance from such streams." He chuckled. "Unlike their descendants, they preferred fishing to hunting wild boar."

I couldn't figure out where Maximus was until I glanced up and saw him standing on a high balcony that was obviously connected to a room on the fourth floor. He was wearing a black robe and a red turban.

"Welcome, Nicolò Zen! You're just in time for dinner. Take a seat, and I'll be right down."

As I approached the table, his assistant entered the room from

 158

a door on my right. She had changed into a black dressing gown and removed the ribbon from her hair, which flowed over her shoulders. She wore silver bracelets on her wrists and a cat's-eye ring on her left hand. "Hello," she said, barely acknowledging me.

"I'm Nicolò."

"I know," she said, sitting down. "I'm Lila."

I took the chair across from her. She moved like Meta—her gestures, her walk—and her voice sounded the same, but up close the resemblance ended. Lila's eyes were narrower, her face more oval-shaped, her lips thinner. Clearly I had projected Meta's features onto her. And yet, as with Maximus and Massimo, there was something about her that made me doubt my own eyes. "It isn't you, then," I murmured.

"Of course it's me."

"I'm Venetian, you know."

She folded her hands on the table and averted her eyes.

"Have you ever been to Venice?" I asked.

"No. Why are you staring at me?" she added crossly.

"I'm a little confused."

"Understandably so," Maximus said, coming up behind me and patting me on the shoulder. "Perhaps by the end of this meal, Nicolò, things will be clearer."

I was startled to see that he had a crow on his shoulder which flew off to a perch across the room and remained planted there.

Maximus's robe was velvet, with a fur collar. His turban was adorned with a pin in the shape of a lightning bolt. As he sat down at the head of the table, Ludwig entered with a Siamese servant girl named Soon-ji. She was wearing a silver sari and carrying a tray of steaming platters on her head. Her long hair was braided down her back. She had bells on her slippers identical to the bells the cats wore on their collars. In fact, she moved like a cat, lithe and self-possessed, with soft, precise steps. She had quick pale eyes, and small alert ears that looked as if they could pick up sounds at a great distance.

The meal she served was unlike any I had encountered in Vienna, or anywhere else: red seaweed garnished with pickled radishes; black rice noodles and spotted mushrooms boiled in wine; grilled squid stuffed with flying fish roe; and yellow cherries sautéed in butter. The hot bread was laced with cinnamon and paprika. The goat cheese was coated with thyme honey. Instead of wine, Maximus drank vodka flavored with pomegranate, which I declined, opting for apple cider. I was already stimulated enough.

Maximus pointed at the crow. "His name is Téodor. He and his brethren outside are from the Carpathian Mountains, near the Laborec River. They are the most intelligent crows in Europe. They can understand human speech and do basic arithmetic. They can even fashion tools with which to build nests. Téodor is the cleverest of the lot. He was a part of my act for many years. On command, he would fly through an open skylight in the theater and bring back some object I had requested: a plum, a coin, a button, a blue or red stone—those are the colors he knows best. Now he is eleven years old, retired, dining on herring and grasshoppers, never confined in a cage. On occasion, two of his sons work with me. But neither is as good as Téodor."

"He can do arithmetic?" I said.

"Téodor," Maximus called out, "how many of us are dining here?"

The crow cocked his head and tapped the wall three times with his beak.

"How many candles does it hold?" Maximus asked, pointing at the candelabra.

Téodor gazed upward, then tapped the wall eight times.

"Excellent, Téodor," Maximus said. "Thank you." Then he turned to me. "Convinced?"

"I am."

"Good," he said, putting a forkful of seaweed into his mouth. Noting that Lila, with downcast eyes, was neither speaking nor eating, he said, "Are you not hungry?"

She picked up her fork and toyed with a radish on her plate.

Maximus turned back to me. "Did you enjoy the performance tonight, Nicolò?"

"It was amazing."

"Comparable to Massimo's performances?"

"I have never seen him perform."

"No? Did he not make it seem as if his beautiful villa were invisible? And perhaps you saw a statue that may, or may not, have come to life?"

I saw Lila was listening more carefully now. "How did you know that?" I said.

"Please. You might as well ask how I knew you were coming here tonight. My brother loves to show off—even more than me—so of course he did that business with his villa. It's one of his favorite tricks."

"Your brother?"

"Yes. And I also have a half brother, Maximiano Grande,

in Madrid, and another, Maxwell the Magnificent, in London. And there are my half brothers Maximiliaan in Amsterdam and Maksim in Saint Petersburg."

I couldn't believe my ears. "All of them are magicians?"

He smiled. "What else would they be?"

"And their assistants?"

"What about them?" he replied, slicing himself a piece of cheese.

"Are they sisters as well?"

"No."

"Why do you ask so many questions?" Lila blurted.

A cold glance from Maximus silenced her. "Nicolò is my guest," he said. "Since you are neither hungry nor convivial, you may excuse yourself."

"What?"

"With an apology . . ."

She was dumbfounded.

"That's not necessary," I said.

But she had already stood up and made an exaggerated bow in my direction. "I apologize," she muttered, and left the room.

"She gets testy after a performance," Maximus said.

"I'm sorry if I upset her."

"It's not you. She's suspicious of strangers."

"When I saw her onstage, she looked quite different."

"Like someone you had met before," Maximus said.

"Yes."

"At Massimo's house, perhaps."

"Then you've been there," I said.

"Not in the way you think." He sat back and sipped his vodka.

"Allow me to tell you a story. Contrary to what people think, magic is more about appearances than mystery: what you see, don't see, think you're seeing, and imagine you've seen. The best magicians are always balancing those four elements, trying to re-order and define reality by way of illusion. The only mystery they pursue is clarification, not obscurity. Mind you, I am not speaking of tricksters and sleight-of-hand artists, but the true magicians who descend in a direct line from the earliest Magi, the Persian astrologers and mathematicians who attempted to unlock the workings of the universe. They spoke a language called Median—passed down from an ancient tribe of that name—which survives to this day among the initiated."

I wondered what he was getting at and why he was so at ease with me, as if I were a long-standing acquaintance and not a fifteen-year-old Venetian exile whom he had known for less than an hour.

"Imagine," he continued, "that a magician had learned of a practice the Median Magi claimed was a commonplace: the ability to create a double. A doppelgänger. In ancient Egypt it was called a *ka*. In the Himalayan Mountains, a *tulka*. A separate entity, with the characteristics and abilities of the original person. Think of the possibilities for a magician: a double of himself, able to appear in two places at once. Emulating the Medians' methods, this magician experimented for over a year, but in the end both succeeded and failed in spectacular fashion. He misread the ancient language, and miscalculated a key variable, and found that, rather than creating a flawless duplicate, he had ended up with two lesser versions of himself. Instead of a man with a double, he became someone who uneasily inhabited two different bodies.

163

Everything about him had been cut in half: his appetites and perceptions, his strength and endurance. He had been diminished, not enlarged. He hadn't even succeeded in imparting his own physical characteristics to the double: there were similarities, but the two could not be mistaken for one another. Putting modesty aside, this man had little doubt that, even so, he was still more powerful than most men at their peaks. And time would bear him out on that."

I felt a chill run through me. "You're talking about Massimo and yourself."

"Am I?"

"Yet you make it sound as if as if it happened to other people."

"I never said it did not."

"So the double became a magician, too."

"Both halves of this man were already magicians. They each continued practicing their profession."

"But in different countries."

"That seemed the wisest course," he said drily.

"Do these magicians ever meet?"

"Never."

"Exchange letters?"

"No." He paused. "Occasionally they can share their thoughts. But that takes a great deal of effort."

"And their memories?"

"Became separate when they separated. Their common memories blurred, and generally disappeared."

"And your half brothers?"

"They really are my—our—half brothers. My father owned a traveling circus, quite celebrated in its time, and had a way with

 164

the ladies. During his long life he had a number of sons all across Europe."

What he was telling me was incredible, but I believed him. I had already seen and heard enough, from him and Massimo, to convince me nearly anything was possible. The world of wealth and privilege to which I had been admitted—however provisionally—astounded me at times, but it was pedestrian compared to the world these magicians inhabited. I had so many questions for Maximus, but they all hinged on one paradox that I would first have to grasp, even if I could not explain it according to the laws of biology and physics: Massimo and Maximus were one and the same man, but they were also separate men.

"Nicolò," Maximus said sharply, bringing me back to myself. "You needed to hear this, but we must move on to the real purpose of your visit here."

"I'm sorry to contradict you, sir, but I came because I discovered this morning that a magician in this city possessed the same name as Massimo the Magnificent."

"It's true that is what brought you to my house," Maximus replied, "but it's not the reason you're here. You've accomplished a great deal in a short time. They're calling you the greatest clarinet soloist in Europe."

"That's my manager's doing," I said, trying to detect irony in Maximus's voice, thinking he must know that I owed my success to Massimo.

"The newspapers seem to agree with Herr Hoyer," Maximus said.

"Do you know him?"

"Yes, he is my business manager as well."

Once again, he caught me by surprise. "So you knew about me before tonight?"

"Yes."

No wonder Massimo had asked Hoyer to manage my career and help me settle in Vienna.

"Hoyer speaks glowingly of you," Maximus went on. "But I didn't know you would be attending my performance tonight." He glanced at my plate. "You're not hungry, Nicolò? Soon-ji will be disappointed to learn that I was the only one to partake of her meal." He raised his glass. "To your health."

The meal was indeed delicious, but I was so busy digesting Maximus's conversation that it was difficult for me to enjoy the nuances of Soon-ji's cooking.

After we ate the cherries, and drank white tea with honey, Maximus said, "You saw the flowers I am tending. They were grown from seeds I received as a gift from a Chinese magician named Yan when he visited Vienna. They can only be found in China, where they're called *mǔdān*. Yan said they would bring me good fortune so long as I maintained one hundred of them at all times. They must be watered with four parts warm water, one part milk, and a teaspoon of cinnamon. Their pollen attracts hummingbirds and butterflies. But it is their petals that are unique. They have the power to enable you to see and hear someone important in your life who is in another place. It ought to be for a compelling reason. The information you obtain may be crucial to you. You must concentrate on this person, and it will be as if you are near them, as an observer, no matter how far away from here they are or what they are doing. So-called clairvoyants claim to

 166

be able to do such things in séances, but that is all a fake. After these flower petals are dried in sunlight, exposed to moonlight, and mixed with seawater, they are boiled down to a smooth liquid. You inhale its vapors and enter a kind of sleep in which you will find yourself transported. That is why you're here," he added quietly. "It doesn't work for everyone: you must be able to concentrate, and also let yourself go. Would you like to try?"

"I would," I said eagerly.

He rang his bell, and Ludwig and Soon-ji appeared, pushing a cart that held a large silver tureen. Engraved on the lid was a bolt of lightning. Ludwig placed the tureen before me, and he and Soon-ji left the room.

Maximus came around beside me. "Have you chosen the person?"

I nodded.

"Breathe," he said, removing the lid from the tureen.

I looked down into a pool of black liquid. A thick, acrid vapor swirled upward. The more I inhaled it, the larger the pool grew and the farther from it I rose, until it appeared to be a lake, then an ocean. The vapor had turned into clouds, and I was drifting through them.

"How long will I be gone?" were my last words to Maximus. If he replied, I didn't hear him, for I was already up in the sky, riding the wind, higher and higher, until the air thinned and my breath grew short, and I began to fall, slowly at first, then faster, through the layers of clouds, to the sea. At the last moment, I closed my eyes, and when I opened them, I hadn't plunged into the water, but to my astonishment was standing on the Riva degli Schiavoni, near the Ospedale della Pietà. I was at the very spot where I had been playing my clarinet for passersby when Luca stopped and invited me to audition for the Master.

I was in Venice, but it was unlike the Venice I knew. I heard the buzz of a crowd approaching on the promenade, but none appeared; heard oars plashing in the canal, where no boats were visible; heard scores of gulls screaming overhead, but saw only a single bird perched on a piling. I smelled fish from the stalls on the fishmongers' pier, but the pier was empty. The statue of *Fortune* atop the Customs House had been replaced by a bronze skeleton wearing a crown. The copper roof was missing from the campanile on San Maggiore. In the colonnade at the Doge's Palace, every other column was gone. I realized, in other words, that large swaths of the city were closed to my senses, their inhabitants as insubstantial as phantoms. The faces of the few people who came near me were blurred. The air was smoky, the light diffused. A ceiling of clouds hovered between the city and the sky. Distances were even more deceptive than usual: the Grand Canal appeared narrow where it ought to have been wide, and the Giudecca had receded, its buildings tiny on the horizon. A cold mist blew in from the Lagoon and burned my eyes. My head ached. I was in a kind of limbo, like the one in which I had made my way to Massimo's villa in the cobbler's blue shoes.

I had not seen anyone enter or leave the Ospedale. I wondered if it, too, was empty. The windows were shuttered. The doors were closed. Suddenly I heard a drumroll, a slow, dull beat from the canal. I saw a gondola approaching from the east. A drummer was standing in the stern with his back to shore. The gondolier had a scarf tied around his face, so only his eyes were visible. His fingers

 168

were long and gray, gripping the pole with which he guided the gondola. A black dog crouched at his feet. When the gondola docked, the drumming stopped. Three people emerged from the small cabin and disembarked: two men in blue coats and hats and a girl in a yellow cloak with long blond hair. They had on carnival masks, the men's blue, the girl's golden, embroidered with silver stars. The men wore scabbards. The handles of their swords were studded with gems. With the men trailing her, the girl walked directly toward me. Her feet barely seemed to touch the ground. The closer she came, the colder the wind grew against my cheek.

When she stopped before me, I saw her blue eyes peering through the mask. Then she pushed the mask up over her forehead. It was Adriana. A little older, slightly taller, and even more beautiful than I remembered her to be. She didn't show surprise or smile. In fact, she showed no sign of recognizing me, unless I counted the momentary look of fear that flashed across her face when, without a word, she produced an envelope from inside her cloak and handed it to me. Then she walked away hurriedly with the men at her heels, heading for the Ospedale. When she reached the doors, they opened without her knocking. A man and woman silhouetted in the darkness, who resembled Luca and Marta, ushered her in and closed the doors behind her. The two men peeled off and disappeared down an alley. The gondola was already gone.

I looked down at the envelope, which was pale blue with a red seal. I was about to open it when my hands and legs began shaking, then the ground beneath me, and everything before me—the Ospedale, La Chiesa, the promenade, and the canal—all of Venice seemed to be turning upside down when suddenly it just evaporated, and I found myself sitting at Maximus's table, flushed, catching my breath, as if I had just traveled a great distance. Yet, though I felt as if I had been gone for hours, in that room only a few minutes had passed. The dinner plates had not been cleared. My teacup was still warm. Téodor the crow was staring at me. But the tureen was gone. And Maximus with it.

Behind me, someone cleared his throat. It was Ludwig, standing in the doorway. "Maximus has retired to his quarters, sir. He told me to bid you good-night and to see you out."

Ludwig led me down another corridor lined with the black flowers. Among the rooms we passed were a library and workroom filled with tools and paints. When we passed the kitchen, I spotted a silver cat perched on a beam above the entrance. She was licking her paws, and the bell on her collar was tinkling softly. She paused to look down at me as I passed, and I was certain I saw a small smile form on her lips.

In the foyer, Ludwig helped me on with my coat, which had been thoroughly dried. When he opened the door for me, Lila surprised me, appearing out of nowhere and taking my arm. "I'll walk you to the street," she said with a wan smile.

The rain had stopped, but water was still dripping loudly from the trees.

Halfway down the path, she whispered, "When you return to Venice, give this to my sister, Meta." She handed me a box, about seven inches long and three inches wide, wrapped in black paper and tied with a black string. Her voice was friendly now, but urgent.

"Then you are sisters."

"Yes, of course. And I am Venetian. My sister and I used to work together. Identical twins can be very helpful to a magician onstage, as you can imagine. When he created his double, one of us had to come to Vienna with him."

"It's true, then."

"Tell my sister we'll be reunited." She glanced back at the door. "Please, there's no time for more questions. Just do as I ask."

"But I'm not planning to return to Venice now."

"Trust me, you'll be returning sooner than you think." She squeezed my arm. "And be careful when you do."

With that, she turned back to the house and I walked to the corner and hailed a cab. I gave the driver Madeleine's address, then sat back and closed my eyes. I needed to regain my bearings.

As my carriage crossed the city, I reached into my jacket for a handkerchief and instead came on the mail I had picked up that day at Hoyer's office: a bill from my tailor and a bank check for my recent recitals. But there was a third envelope, tucked between those two. Pale blue with a red seal, exactly like the envelope Adriana had handed me when I was transported. This time I was able to read that it was addressed to me, care of Hoyer. My heart beat faster, thinking for a moment it might be from Adriana, but the taut, masculine handwriting told me otherwise. The letter, dated two weeks earlier, was written by my old friend Bartolomeo, but it turned out to be about Adriana. In other words, as Maximus had promised, it was essentially a message from the person I had concentrated on.

Bartolomeo wrote:

My dear Nicolò,

    I hope this finds you well. Here in Venice we have heard of
your newfound fame. It does not surprise me, and I am happy for
you. But I am writing to you now with some sadness. Matters have
only worsened at the Ospedale since your departure. Master Vivaldi
is constantly traveling himself now, to Marseilles, Paris, Brussels,
Madrid—anywhere he can stage his operas and make money.
Perhaps he, too, will end up in Vienna. They say he is heavily in
debt. Luca and Marta have the run of the orphanage, and they
have turned it into a prison. In addition to Carmine, they hired two
other porters, who are in fact waterfront toughs. The girls are not
allowed out into the city except to perform. But there have been
no performances. The morale is low. The privileggiate di coro
rehearses long hours, not in preparation for concerts, but merely
to be kept busy. A substitute conductor named Sabato was hired,
whom the girls detest for his arrogance. I took it upon myself to write
to the Master, but have yet to hear back from him. I am writing to
you, however, about a matter much closer to your heart. Adriana
has run away from the Ospedale and not returned. I happened to see
her the afternoon she left, on the bench in the courtyard. She was
preoccupied and fretful. She had a small bag at her feet that she tried
to hide from my view. I pretended not to see it. I asked her what was
wrong, and after some hesitation, she answered that she had learned
by chance that her friend Julietta had not run away, as everyone was
told, but was in Padua in dire circumstances. Adriana would not
elaborate, except to say she felt she must flee the Ospedale and find
her. I warned her how dangerous this could be, and I offered her my
assistance. She refused. Like the other girls, she had learned to be
suspicious of everyone. A few hours later, when the girls were called

to dinner, it was discovered that Adriana was gone. The porters
were dispatched to find her, and I was relieved when they returned
empty-handed, for I would not have wanted her in their clutches for
a moment.

I am sorry to be the one to deliver such news, but I thought you
ought to know. I should add that Adriana asked after you, and I told
her you were in Vienna, making a name for yourself. She wanted
to know how long I had known your true sex. I took the liberty of
telling her some of your story, so she would understand why you had
entered the Ospedale as you did. She knows why you were expelled,
and what you did for her, which moved her greatly. She cares for
you, Nicolò. If I can be of service to you, call on me. I hope we will
see you in Venice again soon. In the meantime, I remain

Your friend,
Bartolomeo Cattaglia

I felt angry and guilty, and most of all, helpless, after reading and
rereading this letter. While I had been gaining fame and riches,
and seeking out pleasure, my friends had been in trouble, and
maybe worse danger than I imagined. I had often rationalized of
late, while enjoying Madeleine's favors and basking in the glow
of my audiences' applause, that I would put my riches to good use
one day, making a triumphal return to Venice and taking Adriana
away from the Ospedale for a better life. It was too late for all that
grandiosity now, but I knew what I must do: settle my affairs in
Vienna as swiftly as possible and travel to Padua. With the time
that had elapsed, I had no idea whether Adriana was there, and if
so, where I might find her. But I had to go.

As I ascended the stairs to the Marquise's apartment, I remembered how certain Lila had been that I would be leaving the city soon. Just how soon, and with what further measure of desperation and confusion, I would find out the moment Madeleine opened the door.

3

"Where have you been?" Madeleine cried. "Noémi's husband is here, looking for us. We must leave Vienna leave at once."

"Her husband?"

"Yes, the Baron told me he arrived this morning. And that he knows about her various affairs, of course, but even worse, that he imagines you are one of her lovers."

"What?"

"It's true. He thinks you have been involved with her, not me. He knows you are a famous musician—that would be enough. Your age would be meaningless to him."

"But who would have told him such a thing?"

"Who knows? You were seen coming and going from here. People gossip. Servants talk. It doesn't take much. The more a rumor spreads, the more it can be twisted."

"But can't you just tell him the truth?"

"Don't you understand, Nicolò? He is furious with us. Noémi left him—forget that it was for good cause—and we have been living on the money she took. He wants revenge. And you have become one of his enemies."

"Where will you go?"

Hurrying around the corner from her bedroom, the Marquise answered my question.

"We will go to Budapest. Somewhere he never goes." She lowered her voice. "You're welcome to join us—for your own safety."

Madeleine took my hand. "Will you come? We were waiting for you."

Over her shoulder, in the parlor, I saw their trunks and suitcases lined up. The Marquise's maid had just entered, carrying her coat. I knew Madeleine was lying: if I had arrived fifteen minutes later, they would have been gone.

She read my expression and averted her eyes. "Honestly. If you didn't come, we were going to go by your apartment."

"We were," the Marquise added, unconvincingly.

I flushed, as much with embarrassment as anger. In the preceding weeks, I had seen how duplicitous the Marquise was, juggling her lovers, but I had expected more of Madeleine. I realized just how much my feelings for her had blinded me. "No, Madeleine. You go."

"You don't know my husband," the Marquise said, pulling on her gloves. "He's a vengeful man."

"You mean he'll challenge me to a duel?"

"No. He's a coward. He'll hire men to beat you. Or worse. That's his way."

Now I did believe her. But after all I'd seen and heard that day, and with so many things happening at once, I wasn't afraid. I just felt numb.

"I'll be all right," I said. "Anyway, I think he'll be more interested in finding you, not me."

The Marquise smiled wryly. "You've learned some things since you arrived in Vienna. Come, Madeleine."

Madeleine hesitated, then embraced me, and despite my

anger and confusion, I held her for a moment, feeling the warmth of her body for the last time.

"There's no time for this," the Marquise said. "Get back to your apartment. Ask Herr Hoyer for assistance. His brother is police commissioner, no?"

"You really think I am in that much danger?"

"I know you are. Now, go."

Madeleine squeezed my hand. "Think of me sometimes, Nicolò."

I looked around the apartment—the sky-blue drapes, the mirrors, the divan by the window—and drew in the scent of all those lilies for the last time. I wanted to tell Madeleine that I would never forget her, but she had already turned away to put on her coat, and I left.

4

The Marquise was right.

When I arrived back at my apartment, I froze when I found the front door ajar. I knew Gertrude would never leave it that way. And for the first time, I was frightened. I could have fled the building at that point, but nearly everything I owned was in those rooms—not the least of which was my clarinet. And I had to make sure Gertrude was all right.

I pushed the door open, and the only light was the glow from a dying fire. I didn't hear a sound. My heart was beating fast as I walked over to the fireplace and lit a tinder stick from the embers. I lit a candle and, holding my breath, slowly made a circuit of the apartment. I didn't come on any intruders, but they had been there all right.

The place was a mess. It had been ransacked, everything turned upside down. Drawers were emptied onto the floor, furniture upended, plates and glasses shattered. My clothes were strewn around the bedroom. And three things were missing: the lockbox hidden in a cabinet behind some books, a pocket watch Hoyer had given me on my birthday, and my clarinet.

My clarinet was gone.

I still didn't believe in sin, and punishment for sin, but at that moment in my apartment on the Braunerstrasse, I had a flash of doubt. I wondered if I was exactly the sort of sinner the priests railed about, the one who rejected God and disdained the Church, and when he was most sure of himself, fell into a pit of misery. I could hear them condemning me—for pride, greed, deceit, and who knows what else—as they made clear that no punishment I suffered would be too great, no misfortune too excessive, unrepentant sinner that I was. I even heard the voice of my former choirmaster, the gentle Father Michele, thundering *Repent, Nicolò, or be damned!*

But I was saved from my doubt, and from further self-pity, when I heard an actual sound in the apartment that terrified me. A scratching and thumping, barely audible, in the closet by the kitchen. I stood outside the closet for several seconds before opening the door slowly and holding the candle up to the darkness. To my horror, I saw Gertrude lying on the floor, her wrists and ankles bound with rope, a piece of cloth stuffed into her mouth, and her eyes wide with fear.

I removed the gag, but only after I had untied both pieces of rope was she able to speak.

"I thought they would murder me."

I helped her up. "You're all right now."

"They broke things, they took things. They shut me in there, Herr Zen."

"Did they hurt you, otherwise?"

"No. Just the ropes," she said, massaging her wrists. "They knocked at the door. I thought it was you. There were two of them, not Austrians."

"I'm so sorry, Gertrude. This should not have happened to you. Come, we're leaving here. We're going to Herr Hoyer's house."

"But your things . . ."

"We need to go now," I said, taking her arm.

She was breathing hard and unsteady on her feet. "Wait. I was able to hide something before they tied me up."

"I don't care about the lockbox."

"Not the lockbox."

I followed her into the kitchen. She leaned down by the oven. "Hold the candle lower, please," she said. She reached into the gap between the oven and the wood bin and pulled out my clarinet.

"How did you manage that?"

"I know it means everything to you."

"Gertrude, I can never thank you enough for this." I took hold of her shoulders and kissed her on the cheek.

She blushed and raised her head a little higher. "I am Viennese. I love music."

VI
Padua

1

I departed Vienna at dawn in a driving rain. The previous days had been tumultuous. Though the Marquise and Madeleine were long gone, her husband, the Marquis, continued to search the city for her—and me—accompanied by his manservant, a former French soldier named Reynal and two local toughs whom Reynal had recruited in a tavern. Reynal himself was more bodyguard than manservant; a battle-hardened man, quick with his fists, handsomely compensated, his principal duty was to keep the Marquis from being assaulted and robbed during his extended casino tours. His secondary duty was to settle scores for the Marquis, a querulous, thin-skinned man who, if the opportunity presented itself, was not averse to committing robbery himself by way of Reynal. For example, on their recent visit to Marseilles, after sustaining heavy losses at the faro table, the Marquis had had Reynal ambush the big winner of the night, drunk on brandy, en route to his hotel and divest him of a thousand francs. Reynal was also adept at menacing or beating various husbands whom the Marquis had cuckolded. In short, they were a rotten pair, and for several days they had focused their attention on me.

Unfortunately for them, what must have seemed a trivial nuisance at most—their menacing and binding Gertrude—became their undoing. For though Gertrude worked at my apartment most of the time, she was an employee of Emmerich Hoyer, and

Hoyer's twin brother, Heinrich, was the police commissioner of Vienna—a chain of connections the Marquis de Montal could never have imagined. And while Hoyer was furious that the home of one of his star clients, an apartment he himself had secured, had been ransacked, what outraged him in a more personal way was the fact that one of his servants should have been frightened and roughed up by three thugs. In order to identify the Marquis as the culprit behind all this, I had to tell Hoyer about my relationship with Madeleine. He took this information in stride—he was surprised, in fact, assuming that because of my fame and success I would have been more precocious with the ladies than in fact I was. That is, he had at first believed that I was indeed one of the Marquise's lovers. And knowing of her many indiscretions, with men young and old, this had not seemed particularly unusual. But he was not so blasé about the Marquis's behavior, and he immediately paid a visit to his brother at police headquarters. To my chagrin, he took me along, and the commissioner, upon hearing my story, cast me a cold glance and nodded, his initial suspicions about me—whatever they might have been—no doubt confirmed, despite the relative innocence of my liaison with Madeleine. Heinrich Hoyer was a policeman through and through, and because I had gotten myself into such a mess, I must on some level have been guilty—of *something*.

"I don't care that he's a Marquis; in fact, I wouldn't care if he were the Dauphin himself: I don't appreciate that this Frenchman has come into our city thinking he can trample on our laws, breaking into houses and assaulting citizens. And now it's clear he has lethal, perhaps murderous, intentions toward our Venetian friend, and this is unacceptable."

He pronounced the word "Venetian" with nearly the same contempt he'd employed for "Frenchman." But, to use his expression, Commissioner Hoyer showed the Marquis his lack of appreciation by having him arrested, along with Reynal and his accomplices, and locked up in a dank cell in the municipal jail. The Marquis raised an enormous ruckus after recovering from his initial stupefaction, but the commissioner did not budge. Not even when the Baron Francke, a well-connected financier, interceded and tried to get the Marquis out. No, the commissioner insisted that the Marquis wait his turn, behind more than a dozen common criminals, before being arraigned before a magistrate during the next session of the court, three days later.

And that happened to be the very day I said goodbye to Herr Hoyer. I had shown him Bartolomeo's letter and shared with him my feelings for Adriana and my concerns about Julietta. He understood, but still tried to discourage me from leaving Vienna. "Your star has just begun to rise," he implored me. "I know people in Venice who can help your friends. You don't need to go yourself." I wouldn't relent, and finally he gave up, and told me to send word as soon as I was ready for him to book me engagements in Venice, Ravenna, Mantua, wherever I liked. He promised that he himself would meet me in Venice in order to make the arrangements. I thanked him, though after what Bartolomeo had written me, performing was the last thing on my mind. After I withdrew a large sum for my expenses, Hoyer and I had transferred the rest of my money—a small fortune of sixty-three-thousand marks at that point—from the Banco del Giro to its main office in Venice, where in our dialect it was known as the Banco del Ziro.

The commissioner had some words of farewell to me, delivered discreetly but firmly at his brother's office: "Think twice, young man, before you involve yourself in intrigues, or it is you who might end up in jail—or worse." I promised I would, thanking him profusely for all he had done.

Then I said my goodbyes to everyone else at Hoyer's office, most especially Gertrude, to whom I insisted on giving a full year's pay.

"I cannot accept that," she objected. "I told you, Herr Zen, I am Viennese—"

"I know, and you love music. Gertrude, you've done more for me as a musician than you'll ever know. Please take the money."

Until Montal and his henchmen were apprehended, I had stuck close to Hoyer's house. I had grown fond of Vienna—in ways I surely would not have had I arrived homeless and penniless, as when I arrived in Venice—and a part of me was saddened about leaving. On my last day in the city, I ventured out to see some of my favorite landmarks one last time. I went to my favorite chocolate shop, and walked under the shade trees in the park by the Danube, and then made my way to the still-unfinished Palais Kinsky, where I watched the masons, high up on their scaffolds, completing the roof of the steeple. Finally, on the spur of the moment, I hailed a cab and decided to ride past Maximus's house as well.

I traveled along the Boulevard Hauser, across the Kirchnerplatz with its green marble fountain, and through the same maze of alleys, which looked every bit as narrow and confusing as they had at night. But when I reached the south end of the Kundenstrasse, my heart sank. I knew I had the correct address, yet between the windowless church and the substation of the

 186

waterworks, there was only a vacant lot, overgrown with weeds, enveloped in mist.

Gone was the black four-story mansion with its iron fence, cobbled courtyard, and broad lawn. There were no signs of a foundation in the damp ground. No footpaths or gardens. All that remained from the night of my visit was the enormous oak tree, but without the crows. I walked around the perimeter of the lot, then crossed the street and closed my eyes and waited a long moment before opening them again. But Maximus's house did not rematerialize, as Massimo's villa had on the Ramo Regina—a "trick" Maximus himself had referred to. Surely this was more than a trick, I thought. Maximus and Lila, Ludwig and Soon-ji, suddenly felt like the figures I saw in that tureen; because they were capable of disappearing without a trace, all of them seemed, strangely enough, to be more vivid, and more real.

It took me ten days to reach Padua. Hoyer hired me a sleek coach, built more for speed than comfort, with two experienced coachmen and four strong horses. The coachmen were brothers, Luther and Fritz, a husky, rough-hewn pair from the farm country of Saxony. They had broad shoulders and large, callused hands. They always seemed at ease, no matter the circumstances, maybe because they knew horses so well. We traveled through driving rain that barely let up, on muddy roads, over steep mountains, stopping only to feed the horses and ourselves and to catch a few hours' sleep. We were detained at numerous checkpoints controlled by Prussian or Bavarian militias. There were frequent skirmishes between these rival forces, the last active combatants in a war that had formally ended the previous year. From the violence I witnessed—captured soldiers summarily hanged, wounded men left to die in fields, villages burned to the ground in cavalry raids—I would never have guessed that a treaty had been signed with great fanfare by two generals who afterward toasted one another's health and took communion from the Archbishop of Pressburg. Twice I had to bribe the guards at checkpoints, and once I was detained for five hours outside a remote village while a corpulent sergeant checked and rechecked my papers and interrogated my coachmen.

When we crossed the border into Venetia, I wanted to kiss the ground. Even the weather cleared at that point, and the final leg of our journey into Padua, through sunlit cornfields, olive orchards, and hilltop villages, passed without incident.

Though it was less than forty miles west of Venice, I had never been to Padua. Of course, until I traveled to Vienna, I had never been outside of Venice at all. That seemed a long time ago now, after I had performed in so many foreign cities. But it had only been fourteen months.

With its red roofs and yellow buildings, marble churches and religious statuary, Padua looked nothing like Vienna. And though it was, in fact, a smaller city, it felt huge to me because my sole purpose in being there was to find Adriana, and I hadn't a clue where to begin. For all I knew, she might have left already. All during my journey, I had fretted about this and tried to formulate a plan of action. Fortunately, a solution awaited me.

Hoyer had suggested a hotel where I ought to stay, where his performers usually went. In writing to Bartolomeo, thanking him for his letter and informing him that I would be traveling to Padua, I had mentioned the name of the hotel, the Ippolito, on the Via Mentana. I arrived at dusk, hungry and weary. At the front desk, the concierge handed me a letter that had arrived two days earlier. It was from Bartolomeo.

> *Dear Nicolò,*
>
> *If you are reading this, it means you are in Padua. I am gratified you've returned to Venetia. I have made many inquiries, and I believe your friend Julietta might be found in the vicinity of the*

Piazza Castello. I regret to say I have no further information about Adriana. Watch out for yourself. I hope we will see you soon in Venice.

Your friend,
Bartolomeo Cattaglia

After depositing my luggage in my room, I went outside to pay Luther and Fritz for their services. It had occurred to me that I might want to leave Padua on short notice, so I invited them to stay on with me at double their usual pay until my business was done. They gladly accepted, and after I asked the concierge for directions, we set out for the Piazza Castello. Bartolomeo's information had raised my spirits, but they were dampened by the concierge's reaction to my query: the Piazza Castello was evidently the nexus of the city's worst district.

As we crossed the city to the Piazza Castello, the bustling, well-dressed Paduans around my hotel gave way, first to a neighborhood of narrowing streets and thinning crowds, and then a succession of arcades lined with cheap shops and shuttered stalls, and finally a network of seedy alleys where pimps and prostitutes, drunks and vagrants, hawkers of stolen goods, and pickpockets setting out on their nocturnal rounds outnumbered working citizens. Realizing how much I stuck out now, riding around in a fancy coach, well dressed myself, I was so glad I'd had the sense to retain the services—and company—of Luther and Fritz. Angry, quizzical eyes peered into my coach from the shadows. The denizens of those alleys would have imagined that someone my age, with those trappings, must be the son of a wealthy businessman

 190

or nobleman. In other words, an easy target. I realized the comfort and luxury I had grown accustomed to in Vienna had dulled my street smarts, otherwise, I would have left the coach behind.

In fact, I knew I had no chance of finding Julietta unless I proceeded on foot. I told the brothers to stop, and explained to them in my fractured German why we were there. They exchanged glances. How on earth, they must have wondered, did I hope to find a single Venetian girl in one of Venetia's larger cities? I described Julietta to them, and said I wanted to walk the perimeter of the Piazza Castello. Fritz would stay with the coach in an alley off the piazza, and Luther would accompany me. I removed my silk-lined jacket and borrowed Luther's spare coat, its oilcloth worn and rain-spattered. To Fritz's amusement, I mussed up my hair as well, and kicked dust onto my boots, and Luther and I set out from the south end of the piazza.

Up close, the dark doorways of the piazza revealed every manner of vice. The first two buildings we passed were obviously brothels, heavily made-up girls in gaudy dresses huddled in gloomy corridors, watched over by dour madams. Holding my breath, I stopped and studied the girls' faces, but Julietta was not among them. Then there was a succession of booths manned by gamesters playing three-card monte and throwing dice. And a large gambling hall where men at circular tables played *cavagnole*, a game in which numbers are drawn from a spinning cage, and *hombre*, a fast-paced game I had witnessed in Vienna, in which cardsharpers are invariably mixed in among the players to gull the unsuspecting. Next came a dance club, dimly lit by red candles, where scantily dressed women performed on improvised stages, often nothing more than a sheet of wood laid on boxes. The

191

music they danced to was out of tune, cacophonous, but none of the leering men crowded four deep was listening to it. I did not see Julietta there, either. Outside all of these establishments, tough-looking men and hardened women were loitering, soliciting for the brothels and the gambling hall. Some of the men exhibited daggers in their belts or leaned on canes that clearly were intended to be used, not for walking, but for clubbing an adversary. These men eyed Luther and me closely, I because of my clothes (despite my attempt at a disguise) and he because of his foreign dress and country gait. Luther eyed them right back with his easy smile, taking stock of their weapons, watching their hands, and following their movements until we had passed. There were wine cellars filled with raucous drinkers, whose brawls spilled into the piazza, and more gambling houses, and another set of booths where Gypsy fortune-tellers and palm readers plied their trades.

At that point, we were nearly three-quarters of the way around the piazza, and I was beginning to lose hope. After all, there were myriad alleys off the piazza; if Julietta was truly in the vicinity, she could be up any one of them. And perhaps, despite his good intentions, Bartolomeo had been misinformed. As we passed another wine cellar and a run-down café, I heard a strain of music wafting from an open door down the nearest alley. I stopped and cocked my ear, for this particular music was actually being played in key, and not badly. It was a lute and a violin. I tapped Luther's arm and led him up the alley. The open door was down three steps. There was a thin curtain immediately inside, and beyond it men's voices, tinkling glasses, and the music. It was another wine cellar, but of a higher quality, apparently.

Pushing the curtain aside, I saw a dimly lit room with maybe four dozen men drinking wine at metal tables. Indeed, they were better dressed than other men I had seen in the piazza. And they were drinking bottled, not barrel, wine. Against the wall, a young man in a brown suit was playing the violin. At first, I could not see the lutist. Then the young man shifted slightly to his right, and there was a girl on a stool playing the lute. She was wearing a white shift. She had long brown hair and downcast eyes. It was Julietta.

I turned around excitedly to Luther. "That's her," I whispered, and he looked even more surprised than me. "I'm sure of it."

We went in and sat down at the nearest table. Luther kept his composure, signaling a barman for a bottle of wine. I saw there were two tall boys at the bar watching Julietta. I tried to catch her eye, but she never looked up. She was pale and thin, and her hair was wild. Her face was so taut, her expression so grim, that it was difficult to reconcile with the girl I remembered.

When they finished playing the song, no one clapped or even seemed to notice. Only then did she look up slowly. For a moment, she glanced in my direction, but showed no sign of recognition. With my hair short, and wearing Luther's coat, I didn't expect her to. There were other boys my age present, but none was sitting with a man like Luther, who, dressed like a farmer, with his healthy tanned face, truly looked out of place. Whatever it was, she looked back at our table, and after a few seconds her eyes widened. I nodded vigorously, and hesitating briefly, she inclined her head toward the boys at the bar. I knew she must be there against her will, and that these boys were keeping a close rein on her.

Luther picked up on all of this. "Go to her," he muttered in German, "and take her outside. I'll deal with those two. Go now."

I stood up and wended my way among the tables. The two boys had picked up on things, too, and were watching me. I strode right up to Julietta.

"Julietta, come with me."

"It's really you?"

"Please, get up."

"I can't. You don't know—"

I took her arm and pulled her off the stool. "Hurry!"

Out of the corner of my eye, I saw those boys rushing toward us, and then Luther heading them off. I made for the door, squeezing Julietta's hand tightly. She was still clutching her lute. Some of the customers cursed at us, but none tried to stop us. Those boys were shouting after us now, and as we pushed that curtain aside, I heard a crash and a loud cry. I turned just as Luther lifted the second boy in the air and threw him against the wall, where his partner was already sprawled out.

We ducked out the door and up the steps. "I have a coach nearby, Julietta. You'll be all right."

"Aldo is here," she said breathlessly. "Those boys are in his gang."

Luther emerged from the wine cellar, where pandemonium had broken out. "Come," he said, and we ran down the alley to the piazza.

"Aldo?" I said to her, and that moment he appeared before us, like a ghost, three other boys close behind him. He was wearing a long coat and carrying a cudgel. Two of the boys were clutching knives.

 194

"Going somewhere, Julietta?" he said.

"Get out of our way," I shouted.

He cocked his head, his blank eyes cast upward. "Am I hearing right? Can that be you, *Nicolà*?"

"Yes, and I could kill you for what you've done to her."

"Kill *me*?" he laughed. "You have it backward. And this little whore will get what's coming to her." He cocked his ear toward his companions, who were describing to him what they saw.

Luther was having none of this. He stepped in front of me, put his fingers to his lips, and whistled so loudly that Aldo jumped back.

"What the hell is that?" he said.

I had never heard such a whistle, which carried clear across the piazza, though his brother was not nearly so far away.

"Stay back," Luther commanded me in German.

"Who's your Austrian friend?" Aldo said, advancing toward us, brandishing the cudgel.

"Come to me," Luther said, standing his ground and beckoning to the three other boys. "Come to me."

They were obviously aware of how he had handled their comrades inside, and they hesitated—just long enough for me to hear a coach approaching on the cobblestones of the piazza.

"What's that?" Aldo said to the boys.

The horses' hooves were echoing loudly. One of the boys turned toward the piazza, the others began circling toward Luther, brandishing their knives before them.

Fritz pulled up at the foot of the alley, leaped from the coach, and ran toward us. He decked the boy beside Aldo with a single punch that broke his jaw, and then pulled down one of the boys with a knife from behind and kicked him in the ribs. Luther made short work of the other one, grabbing his arm and twisting it so hard that, before his knife hit the ground, we heard his wristbone crack like a stick.

"What the hell is going on?" Aldo cried, hearing his companions howling in pain, spinning this way and that, flailing wildly with his cudgel.

"This is for you," I said, grabbing Julietta's lute and swinging it as hard as I could at Aldo's knees. The wood cracked, his legs buckled, and he fell to the street.

"You bastard, I'll kill you!" he shouted as the four of us ran to the coach.

Fritz took the reins with Luther beside him, and Julietta and I jumped inside. As we sped away from the Piazza Castello, I wrapped my jacket around her shoulders. She was shaking. She looked into my face in bewilderment.

"My real name is Nicolò," I said.

She burst into tears. "How did you find me?"

"I'll tell you everything. But, first, I need to know if Adriana is here, too."

"In Padua—no."

"She set out to find you here."

"She's in Venice."

"How do you know that?"

"Because I overheard Aldo say so. His gang has been looking for her. Those other boys are just a part of his gang. They all come out of San Benedicto, the orphanage where he was sent. He enlisted a gang of the worst, most violent boys—so bad they either escaped or were expelled from the orphanage. They steal, they kidnap, they blackmail people. Aldo kidnapped the other girls from the Ospedale, Lutece dal Cornetto and Silvana dal Basso. It sickens me to think where they must have ended up. They kidnapped me the same way."

"From the wine cellar."

"Yes. I'll tell you what happened to me in the last year. I only pray it never happens to Adriana."

3

"Bellona and Genevieve tricked me," Julietta said. "They took me to the wine cellar, saying one of the other girls was in trouble. I should never have believed them. The moment I entered, Aldo and a man in a greatcoat threw a blanket over me, and then tied a rope around the blanket, and carried me out. I put up a fight, but then I felt other hands on me, and suddenly I was in the bottom of a boat. I heard oars dipping into the water. It seemed I was in that boat forever. Then we stopped and they carried me again, and laid me down, and undid the rope. When I threw the blanket off, I found myself in a small, windowless room. It was filthy. Just some straw on the floor where I could sleep, though I barely slept. I was there for several days. Every night someone opened the door and slid through a plate of food with a fork and a pitcher of water, picked up the plate and pitcher from the previous night, and shut the door again quickly. All I saw was his hand. One night I kept the fork. I waited all day, sharpening the prongs of the fork on the stone wall. I waited close by the door, and when it opened and the hand came through, I brought the fork down on it as hard as I could. There was a terrible scream, for the fork went clear through the hand. I yanked the door open, and there was a boy Aldo's age, skinny but tough-looking, clutching his hand. I pushed past him, and for an instant he grabbed hold of my hair, but I pulled free and ran down a corridor, hearing his screams as he pursued me. I heard other voices responding from within the house, and then footfalls as they ran to join him. Suddenly there were two doors before me, on the left and right. I opened the left-hand door and felt a cold wind in my face and saw that I was in an alley. At the near end, I saw people passing on a busy street. I ran there as fast as I could, turned the corner, and was in the Campo Santa Marina, in the Castello. I kept going, in and out of alleys, into the Canareggio, until I reached the Rio della Sensa. It was the supper hour, there were many people about, but still, I stuck out, wearing only my nightdress from the Ospedale. I followed the canal westward and never stopped. You see, I knew where I was going, Nicolò. Prudenza once told me that the convent at the Church of San Girolamo offered shelter to homeless girls. The nuns there are truly pious and will protect any girl who is honest with them about her circumstances. They listened to my story and gave me a bed to sleep in. Their dormitory is not luxurious like the Ospedale's, but it is clean and safe. I was given certain duties, in the kitchen and the laundry, to earn my way. And then, knowing of my musical abilities, they gave me that lute with which you struck Aldo—and I'm glad you did!—so that I could play for them, in the church and in their own dining room. I so feared Aldo and the criminals who employed him that I did not leave the grounds of San Girolamo. Never. But after a year, my fear ebbed somewhat, and I grew restless. I thought I would lose my mind if I didn't go out once in a while. I started by taking short walks. Then I ventured out to the food markets on the Fonda-menta San Girolamo with some of the other girls.

"Finally, just two weeks ago, I grew so bold as to take strolls alone along the Fondamenta di Canareggio. I felt protected there by the crowds, the food stalls, the boatmen milling on the piers. That was my mistake. One day, a member of Aldo's gang was in the crowd, and he recognized me. Maybe it was the boy I stabbed with the fork, or one of the others who carried me off. Whoever it was followed me back to the convent. And the next week, when I went out again, Aldo and four others were waiting for me. They must have come round every day, waiting. They jumped me on the Calle Contarini when no one else was about, and held a knife to my ribs, and forced me into a boat on the Rio della Sensa. After blindfolding me and binding my hands, they rowed out into the Lagoon. After a long time, I realized they were taking me to the mainland. They dragged me from the boat and put me in a cart and brought me to Padua. Aldo beat me that first day and called me every foul name he could think of. He told me that if I ever tried to escape again, he would kill me himself.

" 'You see,' he said, 'even after a year, we found you. And we would find you again. Never forget it.'

"Once I was here, he told me I could make him money by playing the lute or by giving up my body," Julietta sobbed. "And if ever there wasn't enough money from the lute, he would sell me to the first man who asked. In fact, he had me playing in that place to show me off to those men. He was waiting for the highest bidder."

"I'm so sorry, Julietta." I hesitated. "Did he take you to bed himself?"

"No. He touched me as he liked, but not that. And he didn't allow his boys to lay hands on me. He said he wanted me to remain a virgin because he would get more money for me then. And he would have gotten it very soon, if you hadn't come."

She started crying again, and I put my arm around her. "It's all right. You're safe now."

Through the coach window, the city was flying by. I had already decided that we would leave Padua at once. I would pick up my things at the hotel and start out for San Giuliana. We could rest at an inn in Pianiga, halfway to Venice, where Julietta could bathe and dress comfortably, and then continue on at dawn.

"Do you have any idea where Adriana might be?" I said.

Julietta shook her head sadly. "I wish I did. All I know is that we must find her before they do. We don't have much time. After tonight, they'll be looking harder than ever—for both of us."

She was right, and under the circumstances, I knew there was only one person who could help me.

VII
Adriana

1

From San Giuliana, Julietta and I hired a boat to carry us to Venice, and Luther and Fritz set out for Vienna. I thanked them for all they had done—above and beyond what they were hired to do—and rewarded them with a hefty bonus, as I had Gertrude. I was growing accustomed to being wealthy—fabulously so by the standards of my childhood—but I was also aware of my limitations in handling my finances. I had gone from having a few coins in my pocket, when I was lucky, to having a considerable bank account, without the opportunity to learn much in between. I had already been cheated once, and I was fortunate to have an honest man like Hoyer managing my affairs and schooling me in how to do it myself. I think he felt an especial responsibility, not only because of my youth, but because it had been one of his most trusted employees who embezzled from me.

At any rate, no matter how good my intentions, without money I could not have gotten Julietta out of Padua. Or brought her back to Venice. Or been able to buy her new clothes from my old friend Signora Gramani, the dressmaker in San Polo who had outfitted me for my audition.

While Julietta was in the changing room, Signora Gramani looked me over.

"I thought so," she said with a sly smile. "I dressed you once, too, signor—a green dress with lace, as I recall."

"Yes, that was me, I'm afraid."

"I knew, of course."

"How?"

"For one thing, the way you put on your shoes. No girl would do so while remaining on her feet."

"You were very kind, and I've never forgotten it."

"Well, you're finely dressed now, a regular gentleman. But your clothes were not made in Venice."

"I've been living in Vienna."

"May I ask how your fortunes turned around so?"

I told her about my success as a performer.

"Bravo," she said. "And such a pretty girl you've brought here. Is she your betrothed?"

"No, she's a friend."

"Ah," she nodded.

"Not like that."

Signora Gramani lowered her voice. "Does she know you used to dress as a girl?"

"Yes, that's how we met, in the orchestra at the Ospedale della Pietà."

"I see. So you were one of them," she marveled.

"Briefly."

Until that moment, I had no idea where Julietta could stay in Venice. We had both decided it was unsafe for her to return to the convent at San Girolamo, where Aldo and his gang would surely seek her. And a hotel was out of the question. We needed something obscure, out of the way.

"Signora Gramani, you could again do me a great favor—and

this time I can make it worth your while. If it's too much to ask, please tell me."

And that was how Julietta came to occupy the spare room in Signora Gramani's apartment, above her shop. "I always wanted a daughter," Signora Gramani said.

Julietta was only there a few days, but I knew she would be safe, while I myself was entering very dangerous ground.

Knowing I would need more than money and luck to find Adriana, I crossed the Campo San Polo a few minutes later and made my way to the shop of Gamba, the cobbler, on the Calle Filosi.

"Good morning, signor," I said. "You may remember me."

Looking up from his work, hammer in hand, he remained expressionless.

"You once lent me a pair of blue shoes. I wore them when I visited the magician Massimo on the Ramo Regina."

He just stared at me.

"I would like to borrow them again."

He started hammering at the heel of a boot. "If, indeed, you once visited that gentleman, you can return exactly as you are—so long as he doesn't object."

"Are you sure I can find his villa?"

"How should I know? Good day, and be on your way."

I followed the route I had walked the previous year. Except this time, when I turned off the Calle della Chiesa, no mist descended, and the streets did not grow elongated and twist themselves into a maze within a maze. Along the Rio di San Cassiano I passed seemingly ordinary pedestrians: a laundress carrying a basket, a bespectacled old man with his grandson, two nuns fingering rosaries, a sailor eating a pear. The only anomaly was that each of them looked right at me and smiled in exactly the same way—

neither friendly nor unfriendly, just straight, vacant smiles. It was unsettling, but I kept my mind focused on the task before me.

The Ramo Regina was as I remembered it—the four houses, the high wall, the cobbled courtyard—but I held my breath before peering through Massimo's gate. His house was there, all right, completely white, with its tall chimneys and shutters. The marble bench in the park looked the same, but there was no sign of Massimo's statue or its pedestal. As I entered the courtyard, I did see something new at the far end of the park: a pen occupied by a single black pig snuffling in the dirt. I wondered why Massimo would keep a lone farm animal penned up in his elegant garden.

I rapped the front door with the lightning-bolt knocker, and Lodovico appeared.

"He's been expecting you," he said by way of greeting, and took my coat. "This way."

We went to the end of a narrow hallway I hadn't seen before, and he ushered me into a red room: walls, ceiling, carpet, furniture, curtains, candelabra—everything was red. If I tilted my head slightly, the room became one-dimensional, as if I were looking at a red wall, just a few feet away. If I straightened my head again, the room and its contents reappeared, correctly proportioned. I tilted and untilted my head several times, until I grew dizzy.

Then Massimo entered, all in black as before. "Welcome back, Nicolò."

I stood up and shook his hand. "Thank you for seeing me."

"This is part of a new act I am perfecting—are you enjoying it?"

"The room?"

"Yes, of course, the room. But the room is only the spatial

component, it's just the beginning," he said, sitting down opposite me at the red desk.

I tilted my head slightly, and he smiled.

"No, you won't see it now," he said, "so long as I'm present.
Anyway, that's not why you're here."

"I need your help, Massimo. It's important."

"You certainly did need it. And it was important. But now
your friend is safe."

"Adriana?"

"Remember, I know Herr Hoyer well. He holds you in high
regard and he was concerned about you. He dispatched a special
courier with a detailed letter who left Vienna well before you did.
Hoyer told me why you were going to Padua, about Adriana and
your other friend. I trust she is also safe."

"Yes, she's here in Venice."

"Your fears for Adriana were well founded. I intercepted her
before she could leave Venice for Padua."

"But how?"

"Come, Nicolò," he said dryly, "you're not really surprised
that I could pull off such a feat."

"Where is she now?"

"In the safest place in the Republic, outside of the Doge's Palace. My house."

"Adriana's here?"

"She has been my guest for the past week. She will join us
shortly."

I was stunned. "Does she know I'm here?"

"She knew you were coming, eventually. Meta went upstairs

to inform her that you arrived. She is, indeed, beautiful and talented, Nicolò. She played her viola for us one evening. You should know that I have invited her to become one of my assistants."

"You have?"

"Don't worry," Massimo smiled. "She hasn't accepted as yet."

"It would be an honor, I'm sure," I said, choosing my words carefully. "But she is a musician."

"And that's how she would assist me: playing music during my performances. Of course, she might seek employment elsewhere—another orchestra, a chamber group—but it would be a far less rewarding path." He sat back. "As for you, Nicolò, your clarinet has served you well in the world, as I knew it would."

"I will always be grateful to you for that. But we need to talk about it as well."

"All right."

Suddenly it hit me fully that I was soon going to be with Adriana for the first time in fifteen months. I had no idea how she would react. She had never seen me as my true self. I had been one of her girlfriends—a painful thought—with whom she had played music and shared a dormitory, both of us in dresses or shifts.

"Well, what is it?" Massimo asked impatiently. "About your clarinet."

"While journeying from Vienna to Padua, I had a lot of time to think. And I decided it would be best if you removed your spell from my clarinet. That is, I respectfully request it."

I caught the surprise in his eyes. For once, it was I who had aroused *his* curiosity. "Never mind the formalities," he said. "Exactly how did you arrive at this conclusion?"

"One event, in particular, opened my eyes. My clarinet was nearly stolen. Had it not been for one of Herr Hoyer's housekeepers, I would have lost it."

"That would not have pleased me."

"I know. But, in addition, I had to acknowledge that I truly rely more on that clarinet than I rely on myself. It horrified me. Things have come too easily to me. Not just music, but the way I've been leading my life."

"I have heard about some of your adventures, and misadventures."

"I feared that I was becoming corrupt."

"Don't be so rough on yourself. You've suffered your share of hardships at a very early age. Now the world has opened its doors to you. That does not happen to everyone, and it doesn't always happen for long."

"Still, no one gets something for nothing."

"Maybe not. But Hoyer told me how hard you've worked."

"That doesn't make up for the advantage I was given. I don't believe any charade can be as satisfying as true achievement. And I don't want to feel as if I am perpetuating a fraud. My father once warned me that if you benefit from something you didn't truly earn, you will pay a price eventually. Your self-respect, your dignity—maybe even your soul."

"It's ironic that it was your father who gave you the clarinet. Do you think he would have done so if he had been aware of its powers?"

"I don't know. I know he didn't want me to have to struggle the way he did."

"That might have overridden his ethical concerns."

 212

"Whether it did or not, I need to start fresh. On the basis of my own talent, I want to become the great clarinetist others think I am."

"Can you do that?"

"I can try. I must. Surely you understand. You yourself worked tirelessly to become who you are. You told me so."

Massimo nodded. "All right, then. Do you have the clarinet with you?"

"Yes. I always carry it with me now, for fear of losing it. That in itself seems unhealthy."

"You realize that the life you are enjoying now—the fine clothes, the victuals, the freedom to travel and to look after your friends—you may lose all of that."

"Yes."

"Not to mention your fame: it's difficult to acquire, and more difficult to reacquire."

"I understand."

"I hope you do. Put your clarinet on the desk."

As I took it from a pouch inside my jacket, my hands were shaking. Massimo did not close his eyes and deliver an incantation, he did not even touch the clarinet; he merely placed his hands, palms up, on either side of it for about ten seconds, exhaled deeply, and sat back again.

"It's done," he said. "And can never be undone. Good luck to you, Nicolò Zen."

I took back my clarinet. It looked and felt the same, and I was eager to play it. But I felt some trepidation as well, and nervous as I was about seeing Adriana again, that was not the moment to try it out.

Massimo walked to the window, parted the curtain, and gazed out at the garden with his back to me.

"In Vienna you met another magician," he said.

I waited, but he didn't say any more. "Yes, I saw him perform."

"What did you think?"

"Of his performance?"

"What else?"

"Extraordinary. It reminded me of the performances of yours that Meta told me about."

"There are certainly similarities," he said dryly.

"I dined at his house as well."

Massimo turned around slowly. "That must have been interesting." Before I could reply, he said, "Ah, here are the ladies."

Meta entered the room, wearing a red silk dress with long sleeves, a four-tailed dragon embroidered in black on one shoulder, a lightning bolt on the other. "Hello, Nicolò," she said pleasantly.

She was followed by Adriana, wearing a similar dress, but without the embroidery. Against the backdrop of the red room, their skin looked pale and Adriana's blond hair shone. Not surprisingly, she was more tentative than Meta, obviously as dazed as I was by all the redness. A week would hardly be enough time to acclimate oneself to the alternative universe inside Massimo's villa. But when she saw me, her face lit up, and I lost interest in sharing a cryptic conversation about Maximus with Massimo.

Adriana embraced me, and kissed me on both cheeks, and said, "I know what you did for me, and I will never forget it."

"I can't believe you're here."

"You can thank Signor Massimo for that. And Meta, who

214

appeared out of nowhere at the dock in Santa Croce. Though I thought I had done a good job of disguising myself, she came right up and whisked me away minutes before I was to embark for the mainland. It was a miracle."

"No miracle, my dear," Massimo said. "Our friend Nicolò looks well, does he not?"

"He does. They have told me all about your great success," she said to me.

"I have been fortunate. And I feel especially fortunate right now."

"This is indeed a happy occasion," Massimo said. "It's clear you two have a lot to catch up on. And Meta and I have work to do." He opened the door and took a silver bell from his robe. "Lodovico!" he bellowed, ringing the bell. "Prepare the rehearsal room." Then he looked back at Adriana and me. "We'll gather for dinner at seven o'clock."

3

Adriana was more beautiful than ever. Like Julietta, she had grown from a girl into a young woman, taller and with a fuller figure. On the way upstairs, I told her how I had brought Julietta out of Padua, and put her up at Signora Gramani's house, and she started weeping.

"I have been worried sick about her," Adriana said. "Thank you, Nicolò." And she kissed me again.

Massimo had given her a corner bedroom on the third floor that overlooked the Rio di San Cassiano through tall windows. Sunlight was dancing on the water and flooding the room. There were freshly cut roses, red and white, in a vase on the mantelpiece. A sleek white cat was curled up on the bed, and we sat down side by side across from it.

"That's Marco," Adriana said. "He has a sister, Marcella, who is—"

"Silver."

"How did you know?"

"We once met."

Adriana searched my face and touched my hair. "It's so short. You had such lovely hair. It fooled everyone. Or almost everyone, I guess. I knew there was something odd about you. I couldn't understand why I was so attracted to another girl." She blushed. "That never happened to me before."

"Nor I. That is, not while I was pretending to be a girl."

 216

She laughed.

"I had to hold it in," I said. "But perhaps you knew I was an imposter all along."

"I didn't."

"I'm sorry I deceived you."

She shook her head. "I just wish you hadn't gone away."

"I had no choice. And I didn't write to you because I knew all the mail at the Ospedale passed through Marta. I wanted you to know why I went away."

"I understand. When Prudenza told me the truth about you, as you asked her to, I was shocked and hurt. Then I learned what had happened in the wine cellar. And Bartolomeo filled me in on your history." She shuddered. "Where would I be now if they had not admitted you to the Ospedale in the first place?"

"It didn't help that I got myself thrown out."

"On the contrary, you set my departure in motion that very night. You see, after Aldo's expulsion, the Master went on tour, and Marta and Luca did whatever they liked."

"So they were both in on it."

"And Carmine. All of them abetted by Marina and Genevieve, who evidently were rewarded for their treachery by being betrayed themselves, turned over to Aldo's employers, who buy and sell girls, to become their concubines. Without checks on them, Marta and Luca grew increasingly reckless. Another girl, Carmona dal Flauto, disappeared a few months after you left. Then the worst happened. Remember Anita dal Timpano? A skinny girl with red hair. She, too, disappeared one night, and a few days later we learned that she had been found floating in the Rio San Stefano with her throat cut."

"My god. How did you find out?"

"The Contessa Barbera had made a large contribution to the Ospedale, and when she heard about Anita, she returned and put up a stink, demanding her money back. The word was that Aldo and his gang had done it. They kidnapped her, she resisted, and scrawny as she was, they decided she was more trouble than she was worth, and they killed her."

"So Aldo is not just a scoundrel, but a murderer."

"A monster. After I heard of Anita's death, I decided I would run as far away as possible and never go back. We seldom performed anymore, but that week we had a concert at the Palazzo Mocenigo, sponsored by the Duke and Duchess of Alba. My plan was to slip away the moment we finished playing. I plotted it out carefully. I gave a soldi to one of the footmen to find me a boatman who would row me to Murano, where I hoped to hide out in a boardinghouse. Don't laugh, but I planned to disguise myself as a boy and play my viola on the street for money. I thought to myself: if you could do it, I could, too. Then something happened that changed everything for me. The Duke and Duchess have two daughters, and their nanny was watching over them at the concert. An old woman with a hook nose, long white hair, and a limp—I would have known her anywhere. She was my former nanny, Consuela, who had taken me to the Ospedale when my mother's was dying. I had never seen her again, until that night, crossing paths with her in a corridor as I made my way toward the palazzo's pier. It took her a moment to recognize me, but then she threw her arms around me and wept. She said the day she had taken me to the Ospedale was one of the worst in her life. That she had always regretted it, and so on. Then suddenly she took my hand and led me into a parlor where her two charges were sleeping.

"'There is something I must tell you,' she said. 'I've been carrying it around with me all these years. It may come as a shock to you, but no matter.'

"I couldn't imagine what she was talking about.

"'Do you know who your father was?'

"Her question went right through me like a knife, for all my life I had hoped I would be able to answer it. I told her I knew no more than I had the day my mother died, which was nothing.

"'Your father is the Duke of Modena,' she whispered.

"I couldn't believe it, Nicolò.

"'It's true,' Consuela said. 'He was your mother's lover. You are the Duke's daughter, his only living child. His son was killed in the Sardinian war, and his daughter died of scarlet fever just last year. His remaining relatives, his sister, the Baronessa Casina, and her daughter, have practically moved into the palace, but the Duke has kept them at arm's length. Seek him out and reveal to him who you are. I feel sure it will mean a great deal to him—and to *you*,' she added.

"With that, she went back upstairs, and I ventured out to the palazzo's pier, but the footman had pocketed my money and lied to me. There was no boat waiting. I had no choice but to return to the Ospedale with the rest of the orchestra. I bided my time, plotting out how I could travel to Modena and secure an audience with the Duke. I hadn't been so excited in years. The Duke of Modena! That must have been the man I had seen through the window that day, talking with my mother while I waited in the carriage. That is, of course, if Consuela was telling the truth—

and what reason would she have to lie to me after so many years? Then I heard about Julietta's fate in Padua, and I determined that I would somehow help her escape and then go on to Modena to seek my father. You know the rest."

"So you are a princess, Adriana."

"No. Unless he adopts me—which is anything but certain—I am the illegitimate daughter of a Duke. And who knows if he will be as thrilled to meet me as Consuela thinks. Anyway, I have begun to have my doubts about the whole matter. I am more fearful than hopeful. I sent two letters to the Duke of Modena, requesting an audience, identifying myself by my mother's name, but I've received no reply. Either it is not true, after all, or it is true, and he wants no part of me."

"Or his sister the Baronessa is intercepting your letters." I had been around aristocrats in Vienna long enough, hearing their tales of court intrigue, to know that this was the likely answer.

"Yes, I know, like Marta. Even so, I have no idea if the Duke was aware that I was at the Ospedale, or if he ever made an effort to find me. I don't know if he's a good man, warmhearted or cold. I don't know anything about him."

"I will get you in to see him," I said boldly.

"You? But how?"

Even as she related all this to me, I was hatching a plan, but I didn't want to share it with her just yet.

"Trust me, I will do it."

She took my hand. "I do trust you, Nicolò. I can't think of anyone I trust more."

She leaned closer and kissed me on the lips this time. I embraced her and breathed in her scent. It was the happiest I had felt in a long time. Then a darker thought crossed my mind. I looked around the pretty room and saw more beautiful clothes hanging in the closet and an array of perfumes on the dressing table.

"Massimo told me about his offer to you. Are you really thinking about becoming one of his assistants?"

She shook her head. "I considered, but not for very long. I am a musician, not an accompanist. Moreover, I need to go to Modena. That is what I want to do, first and foremost."

"Good."

"I'm glad you agree," she smiled.

"Have you shared with him what your nanny told you?"

"No. You're the only one I've told."

"Let's keep it that way until we get to Modena."

4

After dinner, we were drinking Massimo's burdock tea when Lodovico brought in a plate of candied truffles.

"These truffles come from my own garden," Massimo said, putting one in his mouth. "You may have seen the pig that digs them up for me."

"He wasn't here the last time I visited," I said.

"No, he is a new addition to our household. However, he was once someone you knew, Nicolò—before he was a pig. An exceptionally greedy individual, who, true to form, resorted to stealing. In fact, he stole from you."

A chill ran through me. "Stefan?"

"He wanted riches: he can dig for them now, with his snout." He ate another truffle. "They are an expensive food, and he provides a steady supply."

Adriana had no idea what he was talking about, but Meta did and, averting her eyes, didn't say a word.

As Lodovico refilled our teacups, Adriana, politely but firmly, told Massimo she would be eternally grateful for everything he had done, but had to decline the offer of becoming his assistant.

Massimo's face darkened. "You're sure?"

"Yes. There are matters I must attend to. Perhaps one day I will join an orchestra again."

Massimo was annoyed, but anticipating this, Adriana added

smoothly, "I do know of someone who would make an ideal assistant, and I believe she would jump at the opportunity."

I looked at her quizzically.

"My dearest friend, Julietta, whom Nicolò has brought back to Venice. She is a talented musician on several instruments and very poised. Is that not true, Nicolò?"

I nodded agreement.

"How can you be so sure she would be interested?" Massimo asked.

"Because I know her as well as I know myself."

Massimo turned to me. "Where is this Julietta now?" he said impatiently.

"Not twenty minutes from here."

"All right, then, go fetch her."

"Now?"

"Yes, now," he said impatiently. "The sooner I know, the better. Meta will accompany you."

Meta looked surprised, but excusing herself, went to get a shawl.

"Of course I'm disappointed, Adriana," Massimo muttered, "but I wish you the best. So you'll be leaving here soon."

"Yes."

"With Nicolò, I expect."

We exchanged glances, and she smiled. "Yes, he will be with me."

"Well, then, don't linger, Nicolò. I'll have Lodovico brew more tea. And while we await your return, perhaps Adriana will favor me with one of Master Vivaldi's sonatas on her viola."

5

It was past ten o'clock when Meta and I set out. It was a dark, cloudy night, and the streets were nearly deserted.

Leaving the house, I glanced toward the small park. "Is that really Stefan?" I said. "Can Massimo do that?"

"He can do much worse than that," Meta replied. "He is fond of you. And it's clear you're more worldly than the last time you visited. But never let down your guard with him."

Before we turned off the Ramo Regina, I reached into my pocket. "I brought you something. From your sister."

She took the box and searched out my face in the gloomy light. "From Lila?"

"She gave it to me just before I left Vienna. She asked me to tell you that you and she would soon be reunited."

"She said that?"

"Those were her exact words."

"Excuse me a moment, Nicolò," Meta said, turning her back on me and walking a few steps away.

I heard her unwrap the box, and gasp when she opened it. Then she stood still for a long moment, slipped something inside her cloak, and returned to me. "Let's go," she said, and it was clear she wasn't going to reveal the contents of the box.

We proceeded toward Signora Gramani's house, but had gone

only about twenty paces when a cluster of shadows against a wall came to life and several cloaked figures rushed toward us.

"It's her!" one of them called out.

"Get him first," another ordered.

They were all over us in a matter of seconds. Six boys—the tallest of them remaining in the shadows, spitting out orders.

"Bring her here," the tall one said.

I recognized that voice.

"Let go of me!" Meta cried.

"You're sure it's her?" Aldo asked.

"It's her, I tell you."

"It is," another boy called out.

Meanwhile, one of the others put me in a vise hold from behind, pinning my arms back, while his partner pummeled, first in the body, then swinging wildly for my head.

"Leave me alone!" Meta screamed.

Three of them were dragging her to the wall where they had been hiding, waiting to jump us. Two of them pinned her arms while the third put his hands around her neck and began choking her.

"Help me!" she screamed before her breathing was cut off, but now that the boy punching me had bloodied my lip and knocked the wind out of me, the two of them were holding me fast and watching the others.

"Now you can watch your Adriana die slowly," Aldo laughed, "and still be able to say goodbye."

"Adriana?" I gasped.

"Don't try to bluff me. All of these boys saw her before, and now they recognized her at once. After tonight, no one will ever see her again."

"You're making a mistake, Aldo."

"No, you're the one who made a mistake," he said, limping toward me, supporting himself with a cane. "I have to use this because of what you did to me." He raised the cane and brought it down on my head.

He's going to kill me, too, I thought, and when they're done, they'll drop us both into the Lagoon.

Then I heard Meta scream again, just as Aldo was raising his cane a second time. And through the blood pouring down my forehead I saw that she had somehow broken free of one of the boys. Her dress was torn off at the shoulder, and she was scratching the face of the other boy. He pushed her against the wall and began hitting her, and the other two boys joined him, raining down punches.

I closed my eyes, awaiting another blow myself when suddenly I heard a different scream altogether: it was one of the boys attacking Meta. A terrible shriek, followed by another, from the other boy, and as they both fell away from her I saw the flash of a knife in her hand as she plunged it into the boy who had tried to choke her, who cursed loudly and grabbed his chest.

It all happened so fast that the two boys holding me were stunned into releasing their grip. And Aldo was shouting over the groans and shrieks of the wounded boys, bewildered again as to what was happening. By then there had been enough noise to rouse even the most reluctant samaritans, and we heard shouts and footfalls as they hurried toward us from down the street.

 226

The boy who had been holding me took Aldo's arm. "We have to leave," he said. "The girl had a knife."

"A knife?"

"Jerome and Claudio are bleeding badly and Marco looks dead."

"That girl—it's impossible."

"Hurry, people are coming. I hear a constable."

Aldo cursed me, and cursed them, and the three of them disappeared around the corner. I wiped the blood from my face and staggered over to Meta. I felt a huge bump rising on my skull. I thought I was going to pass out.

She was slumped against the wall, her lip and cheek cut, blood matting her hair, and a welt rising over her eye. I took off my jacket and draped it around her before the constable and several other men arrived. She held up the bloody knife.

"This is what Lila sent me."

"What?"

"This was in the box you brought. Don't you understand? It's so I would have it now, when I was attacked."

"How—"

"Don't ask how. Believe me, that's what just happened." She wiped the blood from her lip. "You were right: they made a mistake."

6

After we returned to Massimo's villa, and I told him what had
happened, after he tended to Meta's wounds and Adriana took
her upstairs to bed, after he had Lodovico put a compress on my
head, give me a vial of herbs, and draw me a bath, Massimo stood
before me wearing a black greatcoat, hat, and boots. His collar
was turned up and he was pulling on a pair of leather gloves. He
had listened to me earlier without saying a word, his face set in a
kind of grim fury, while Adriana wept at the sight of us. He still
had few words for me, but if anything, his anger had intensified.
I could feel it emanating from him, as I would feel a wave of heat
or cold.

"How is your head?"

"I'm all right. And Meta?"

"I gave her something to sleep. You will sleep here tonight.
Do not leave the house. Lodovico's prepared a room."

"I wish I could have done more out there."

"Outnumbered as you were, it was enough that you brought
her back. I'll be out for a while. Get some rest."

Without another word, he walked down the hall. I discovered
that he had given me something to sleep as well, in the form of
those herbs, and within a few minutes of Lodovico's turning down
my bed, I was fast asleep.

Just after dawn I came downstairs and found Massimo sitting

228

alone in the drawing room in a red robe, sipping burdock tea, an open book in his lap. It was a bright sunny morning. Light was pouring through the windows and birds were singing in the garden.

"Tea?" he said, pouring me a cup.

He looked as calm as could be as I sat down across from him. I strained to see what he was reading.

"The girls are still asleep," he said. He indicated my head.

"It's better," I said.

"Are you well enough to complete your errand of last night?"

"To get Julietta?"

"Lodovico can accompany you, if you like."

"No, I prefer to do it myself."

"Good." He picked his book up again. "We'll have breakfast when you return."

He was reading Petrarch's *Sonnets*.

7

I followed the same route Meta and I had taken the previous night. When I came to the trees beside the wall where Aldo and his gang had been hiding, I examined the ground. There were signs of a scuffle, and several patches of blood dried a darker brown than the soil. Aldo's companions had seen Adriana before. They expected her to be in my company, and so it was her visage they projected onto Meta as we approached. If it had really been Adriana, they would have raped and killed her. Meta had honed many arcane skills while assisting Massimo: how to leverage her weight, escape restraints, suppress fear, operate in darkness, and luckily for me, how to wield a knife.

Most of that blood belonged to the boy the others called Marco, who had indeed succumbed to his wounds and been carted off by the constables. The other five boys had escaped into the night.

I wanted to clear my head, which was still throbbing from the blow Aldo had dealt me, and I decided to take a detour on the way to Signora Gramani's house. I walked to the Grand Canal and stopped to drink in the wind off the water. Everything felt fresher there: the light was clearer, sounds were muffled. I followed the Fondamenta de l'Ogio past the fish market, where the fishmongers were donning their aprons; and the produce stalls, where the farmers from Chioggia were arriving on barges; and the boathouses on the Calle della Pescheria, where the nocturnal fishermen were sorting their catches. All seemed orderly and pleasantly routine until I rounded the bend at the Mercato di Rialto and heard a great commotion at the foot of the Rialto Bridge. A small crowd had gathered, shouting and pointing upward. It took me a moment to focus, gazing up into the glare of the eastern sky, but when I did, I thought the blood in my body had stopped flowing and then rushed on again in a torrent, making me reel.

From the underside of the bridge, five bodies were hanging by their necks on long ropes, swaying slowly. Gulls were wheeling overhead, screaming, but it was a flock of crows that had alighted on the shoulders of the corpses, pecking at their faces, agitating the crowd all the more. Only when I reached the edge of this crowd could I could confirm what I had immediately suspected: it was Aldo and the four members of his gang suspended over the canal, their necks broken and their faces reduced to bloody pulps. The crows had yet to pluck out Aldo's blank, milky eyes, but I would be lying if I said I felt a shred of pity for him at that moment.

8

Two days later, Adriana and I departed Venice for Modena, a journey of one hundred miles. In the meantime, a good deal had happened. Julietta agreed to serve as Massimo's assistant. After her ordeal in Padua, and with slim prospects as a musician, she was thrilled to be asked. Meta would stay on at the villa until Julietta was sufficiently trained. After that, Meta planned to move to Vicenza, to begin a new life. Without hesitation during her convalescence, Massimo had granted her request to be reunited with Lila, whom he had sent for in Vienna.

"You have worked tirelessly for me, without complaint," he said. "I promise that you and your sister will never want for anything."

I knew he was disappointed about losing Adriana's services—and company—but our enlisting Julietta, and her obvious enthusiasm, seemed to have mollified him.

The sensational deaths of Aldo and the four members of his gang had become the talk of the city. When I arranged to meet Bartolomeo at his sister's house, he greeted me with a bear hug and then looked over my well-tailored clothes.

"Quite an improvement since the last time I saw you," he said dryly.

I thanked him for alerting me to the plight of Julietta and Adriana, and filled him in on what had transpired since I left

Vienna. Signora Botello again treated me like one of her long-lost sons, who were still on active duty in the Ionian Sea. When she said she didn't approve of how thin I looked, I appreciated the irony: a diet of rich Viennese food and enjoyment of the finer creature comforts had left me less robust than when I was surviving on scraps. She insisted I share their supper of fish stew, grilled eel, and pickled radishes. "And plenty of bread basted with oil," she added.

Bartolomeo told me Aldo had been suspected of numerous robberies and assaults, kidnappings, and at least one murder, but the constables had never been able to catch him red-handed or find witnesses who would talk. Interrogated by magistrates from Castello and the Dorsoduro, and once by a State Attorney who could have thrown him in prison on the spot, he fell back on his blindness to elicit sympathy. How could a blind orphan, he declared, who relied on charity and goodwill, be responsible for so much mayhem? "I can barely dress myself," he would whine, "much less wield a knife or club."

"For a time, it worked," Bartolomeo said, slicing the bread. "But when Aldo learned that a captured member of his gang was willing to testify against him, as well as Marta and Luca, and that the police had secured warrants, he fled to Padua and Marta and Luca disappeared—probably to a far more distant place. I am surprised Aldo returned here at all. He had made many enemies, honest and crooked." Bartolomeo looked at me from under his thick eyebrows. "Someone he crossed caught up with him—with a vengeance. He wasn't just killed: he was executed."

Though those of us residing in Massimo's villa felt sure we knew the identity of Aldo's executioner, we did not dare broach the subject with Massimo. What could we have said? Adriana, Julietta, and Meta evinced as little regret as I had over Aldo's fate. They did not personally witness the gruesome spectacle at the Rialto Bridge, but knowing of his various crimes, and of the damage he had intended to inflict on them, I doubt even that would have softened their hearts.

As for Massimo the Magnificent, I would always feel conflicted about him—not surprising, since literally and figuratively, he was a man split in two. He could be a beneficent force, using his considerable powers and connections to help the likes of me, a poor boy who had come to him out of nowhere. I owed him a great deal, and perhaps for that reason trusted him more than he might have expected. He was also the most terrifying and enigmatic man I ever knew. Even those he cared about—perhaps us most of all—were frightened of him because we knew what he was capable of and sensed that he only revealed a fraction of those capabilities.

On that last day, after Lodovico had loaded our baggage onto a cart, and Adriana and I had said our goodbyes to Julietta and Meta, Massimo took me aside in the courtyard.

"You have not yet tried to play the clarinet again, have you?" he said.

"You know I haven't."

"Any regrets?"

"None."

"Fears?"

"Some."

"And what is it you most want now?"

I indicated Adriana, awaiting me beside the cart.

He nodded approvingly. "You're very lucky, Nicolò—maybe more than you know. Many of us don't seize the moment when we meet the right partner. We assume there will be other such moments." I was surprised, for however oblique, this was the most personal revelation I'd ever heard from him. "I will share with you something my old mentor, Hajik Nassim, once told me," he went on. "Remember it well: 'Those who truly guide you in life do not show you where happiness lies, but where it doesn't.'"

VIII
Modena

1

We traveled for three days, mostly on the road south originally built by the Romans in the time of Augustus Caesar. Once we were past Padua, broad yellow fields opened up on either side of us. Farmers were cutting the tall hay, the sun reflecting off their scythes. Women with kerchiefs round their heads and baskets on their backs walked alongside the road. The baskets were filled with cucumbers or tomatoes or ears of corn. The sky was a radiant blue, cloudless, almost painful to stare at.

With Adriana beside me, I felt at peace with myself for the first time in a while. Though she tried to remain cheerful, I could see she was preoccupied, anxious about the reception she would receive in Modena, wondering if she would be received at all. I really did have a plan. It was quite simple, really, and rather ingenious—or so I told myself. If her request to see the Duke was rebuffed by his retainers, I would, without mentioning Adriana, present myself at his palace alone and tell them that I would be pleased to give a recital, at the Duke's pleasure, to honor his love of music. I had learned of the latter by making a few inquiries before we left Venice. Albinoni and the violinist Coletti had performed at his court, and the Duke himself played the clavichord and fancied himself to be rather proficient. I was not being immodest when I thought there was a good chance my reputation might have preceded me as far south as Modena. I really had gained a good measure of fame in Vienna, and throughout Austria and Bavaria, and as Herr Hoyer often told me, I was not only the foremost clarinet soloist in Europe, and a prodigy, but was also a pioneer of sorts on the instrument. Should I require it, I also had a letter from Herr Hoyer to the musical director at San Angelo in Venice. I was supposed to deliver this letter in person, but I had held on to it in case I was asked for a formal reference. At any rate, if, as I expected, the Duke invited me to perform for him, I would take Adriana along and at the appropriate moment introduce her to him. It might be awkward at first, but I hoped that, seeing her face to face, he would be more receptive to her than his silence with regard to her letters might indicate. At any rate, she would be able to address him directly. I couldn't, of course, extend my planning beyond that point.

Of course, all of this entailed getting into the Duke's good graces, and that meant entertaining him properly with my clarinet. When I told Massimo that I had no regrets about the clarinet's having been restored to its original state, I was telling the truth, for all the reasons I had first given him. But on the day he acquiesced to my request, I had no idea I might be giving a recital on which Adriana's happiness hinged. The timing was unfortunate. I knew the first performance I gave after the clarinet was altered was going to be a challenge. The closer we got to Modena, the more I asked myself why it had to be this one, putting that much more pressure on me. All my bravado to Adriana about making things right suddenly rang hollow to me.

As if reading my mind, she took hold of my arm at that moment and rested her head on my shoulder. "Everything is going to be all right," she said. "It's not going to do any good for me to fret about it."

Nor I, I thought, and a few minutes later she had drifted off to sleep.

2

That first night we put up at an inn in the town of Lendinara, beside the Adige River. A night I would never forget. Of course Massimo had given us separate bedrooms while we were his guests. This would be the first time we shared a room. At first, Adriana seemed to have no qualms about this. She acted as if it was perfectly natural. As for the innkeeper, he eyed us skeptically until I asked for his best room, and without hesitation paid him in advance the inflated amount that came off the top of his head. I signed the guestbook *Signor & Signora Nicolò Zen*. Then the innkeeper picked up our bags and led us upstairs and told us our supper would be ready whenever we were.

We ate roast chicken and potatoes at a table by the window in the small dining room on the first floor. There were two men drinking wine at the bar, and a table with an old married couple. From across the field behind the inn we could hear roosters crowing and donkeys braying. I asked for wine and the innkeeper's daughter filled two goblets with dark wine from a barrel. When she served them, she looked us over, especially Adriana's white dress, which had been a gift from Meta. The girl was our own age—Adriana had just turned sixteen and I was several months short of it—and she was clearly curious about why a seemingly affluent couple would have stopped at a country inn when they were only a few hours from Ferrara, a city with luxurious accommodations.

Only when we returned to our room did it seem to hit Adriana that we were going to share a bed. Later she would tell me that the fact we had been dormitory mates at the Ospedale was what had made it all seem so natural to her. I'm not sure I believed her completely—not because she would lie to me, but because it really *did* seem natural, though being dormitory mates and being lovers were not comparable.

And it was lovers that we became in that room, after standing by the window to gaze at the stars. We were both nervous when we sat down on the edge of the bed—I less so after my liaison with Madeleine Pellier to whom I was grateful at that moment. But when I took Adriana in my arms and we kissed, it felt very different than it had with Madeleine. I was excited in the same way, and eager, but I was not just infatuated with Adriana, I was in love with her.

Modena is a smaller city than Padua or Ferrara. At its center is the enormous Duomo, a cathedral built on the tomb of the city's patron saint, Geminianus. Along its north end, also enormous, is the Palazzo Ducale. At that time, it was debatable which of the two was more important in the life of the city: the Church, headed by a distracted archbishop ambitious to become a cardinal and leave Modena for Rome, or the State, which was synonymous with an equally ambitious Duke whose sole focus was Modena, which he wanted to make as influential as the cities to her east and west, Bologna and Parma.

Rinaldo d'Este—Rinaldo III—was the Duke of Modena. The d'Este line was long: at one time, Rinaldo's ancestors had also held the title of Duke of Ferrara and controlled the two large, rich provinces on either side of the Panaro River, an area of roughly sixteen hundred square miles. Now all that remained of that domain were two outposts, the principalities of Mirandola, twenty miles to the north, and Casina, ten miles to the south. The latter, the poorer of the two, was nestled high in the Apennine Mountains and ruled by the Duke's sister, Beatrice, the Baronessa Casina. Her father had married her off to Barone Casina, a fading aristocrat who received a large dowry, in order to consolidate Modena's hold on the principality. The Baronessa had been widowed young. Because she and her daughter, Maria Angela, were his only remaining blood relatives, the Baronessa was maneuvering to have the Duke anoint Maria Angela as his successor in Modena. To date, he had resisted her entreaties, but the Baronessa was certain she would convince him. She reasoned that he had no choice, after all, unless he remarried at the age of sixty-two and fathered another child. But that was unlikely; he seemed to be frozen in deep mourning and perpetually gloomy. Preceding the deaths of his children, Rinaldo d'Este had lost his wife, Charlotte Felicitas, four years earlier. In retrospect, that was the worst blow of all. When it came to running the government, however, the Duke remained strong-minded and intellectually sharp, well attuned to his citizens. He didn't suffer fools, and he was not easily deceived or outmaneuved. Having ruled for four decades, he knew how to inspire both loyalty and fear. He spent even more time in his library and liked to entertain visiting scholars. But, as always, the concerts and recitals he sponsored at the palace were his greatest pleasure. There were intimate evenings for members of his court, local gentry, influential bankers and merchants, but also frequent performances open to all that his late wife had preferred, which were staged in the great hall of the palace.

Adriana and I entered Modena on a warm afternoon and found a hotel near the palace. I requested a room on the top floor in the rear, where I could play my clarinet without disturbing anyone, and they accommodated me.

It was an expansive room that overlooked a narrow, little-used courtyard. It had a large bed, a washbasin and pitcher, heavy drapes, and a Persian rug. Curling her toes in the thick rug, Adriana sat down on the edge of the bed. I had grown accustomed to hotels during my tours, but she had never stayed in a large urban hotel. I hung up my jacket, washed my hands and face, and took my clarinet from its case.

"What are you doing?" Adriana asked, removing her stockings.

"I need to practice."

"Come here," she said, holding out her arms.

I walked over and she pulled me onto the bed.

"I need to practice, too," she said, blushing, and we burst into laughter.

 246

4

Adriana was asleep two hours later when I put on a robe and took up my clarinet. This was the first time I would play it since Massimo had returned it to its original state. I was still nervous, but with all the turmoil of late, I was glad I had waited.

I raised the clarinet to my lips, wet the embouchure, placed my fingertips on the keys, and blew a middle D. Then E, F, G, up the scale and back to D. I waited a few beats, then launched into the opening bars of Corelli's Sonata no.4, a piece I had performed many times, written for the flute but easily transposed to the clarinet. Concentrating on each measure, I tried as always to hear it in my head first; but now, instead of leading me, the clarinet was following; instead of offering cues, it was taking mine. I was rusty, and for the first hour terrified that I was sounding worse and worse. But gradually I relaxed—something I had taken for granted as a performer—and once I realized I could relax enough to block out my fears, my playing improved. In fact, I sounded better than I expected. Even while empowering me as a performer, the clarinet had been teaching me, honing my technique, pushing me toward perfection by enabling me to play nearly perfectly.

Still, I was wary. Perhaps because I had been relying on the powers of the clarinet more than I needed to (which had never occurred to me), I may have grown accustomed to holding back, deferring my own instincts, however rough or eccentric they might be. It was a conundrum: because I had played so well, on a newly invented instrument, people had considered me unique and rewarded me with enormous attention; yet, now that I was on my own, I worried that my playing was not only less polished, but not nearly so unique. Listening to myself that morning, I was awfully hard on myself and thought I sounded like any number of wind musicians, which had certainly not been the formula for my great success. Perhaps what was missing, I told myself, was not so much Massimo's magic as my own soul.

I didn't know how long Adriana had been lying awake, listening to me practice, when she said, "Are you going to let me in on your plan? I think I need to know."

"Yes, you do."

I sat down on the bed and laid it out for her in detail. She listened carefully, nodded in agreement several times, and then said, "Haven't you overlooked a certain possibility?"

"What do you mean?"

"Instead of my accompanying you to the palace and joining the audience while you perform, how about if I accompany you on the viola instead?" She smiled. "I'd like to have a hand in seizing my own fate."

 248

5

Early the next morning, I walked over to the Palazzo Ducale. The palace is an imposing, elegantly designed building of pale stone, with tall windows and ornate balconies and balustrades. Three stories high, with a tower at either end and a spacious rectangular rotunda crowned by a clock steeple, it had a marching green that could accommodate two battalions and elaborate gardens in the rear containing three fountains, an arbor, and a two-hundred-foot reflecting pool lined with statues of angels and demons. Oddly, many of the demons had angelic faces and most of the angels looked demonic. Gargoyles jutted from the eaves of the towers.

Four guards in red and black uniforms flanked the entrance. They admitted me to an anteroom where two clerks were sitting behind imposing desks. I handed one of them a letter I had written to His Grace, Rinaldo d'Este, Duke of Modena, and asked that he kindly deliver it.

"Are you a citizen of Modena," the clerk asked, "and this a request or complaint of some sort? If so, you must—"

"Please tell him, sir," I interrupted, "that Nicolò Zen of Venice, the clarinetist, would like to honor him with a performance, if it pleases him. The letter explains the rest. Thank you."

I walked out without another word. I thought this was the sort of tone, proper but firm, to which a palace functionary would respond. Adriana and I ate lunch at a restaurant on the Via

Caselle and then strolled through the nearby park. She liked to feed the birds, and took some bread crumbs from the restaurant that she tossed them. When we returned to our hotel, I hoped to find a note from the palace awaiting us, but there was nothing. We spent the afternoon practicing an assortment of sonatas by Corelli, Albinoni, and our former Master, Vivaldi. The viola and the clarinet made for an interesting pairing: we had to imagine the accompaniment of other instruments, ideally a violin and a cello. I was still somewhat hesitant on the clarinet, unsatisfied with the fluidity of my sound, but when I mentioned this to Adriana, she insisted I was playing beautifully. Maybe so, and I just couldn't hear it properly; or maybe she was keeping up my spirits. Either way, playing alongside her was a blessing and relieved some of the pressure I felt. I also enjoyed the intimacy of playing alone with her, just for ourselves. When we simply could play no longer, we had supper in the hotel dining room and then fell asleep in one another's arms.

We were awakened at dawn by a knock at the door. I pulled on my pants and opened it to the concierge, who, clearly both impressed and frightened, handed me a gold envelope.

"From the Palazzo Ducale," he said unnecessarily, for affixed to the envelope was the official red wax seal of the Duchy of Modena.

I tore the envelope open the moment he was gone, and got back under the covers. Adriana sat up sleepily.

"It worked," I said. "He says, 'My cousin, Count Cecci of Torino, after attending your performance in Strassburg, raved about it. I am delighted to learn that you are in Modena.' Then he invites us to perform at the palace the night after next. He will provide a violinist and a cellist from his State orchestra."

She hugged me. "I can hardly believe it. You're so clever, Nicolò."

Maybe too clever, I thought, concerned more than ever about the quality of my own playing now that this scheme had become a reality. Now that both Adriana's future and my own were riding on it. "I'll send down for a pot of tea," I said. "We need to practice some more."

6

On the appointed night, Adriana put on a white dress and silver shoes we bought the previous day, combed out her long blond hair, and looked serene as could be, though I know she was anything but that on the inside. I wore a black suit and new black boots. I was edgy, but my nerves had settled down. It wasn't so much that I felt more confident as that I had learned in Vienna how to shut the world out and turn inward at such times in order to calm myself.

As we approached the Palazzo Ducale, carrying our instruments, we stopped to gaze over the rooftops at the half moon rising against the dark blue evening sky. Then we turned around and Adriana stared hard at the palace. We had passed it several times since arriving in the city, but the prospect of entering it obviously gave her pause.

"It looks enormous," she said. "All those lighted windows— how many people do you think are in there?"

"The Duke has a large court. And there will be other visitors, come to hear the music."

"You're accustomed to this, Nicolò, performing in all those big concert halls. I'm used to playing behind the grille at the Ospedale, not standing on an open stage."

"You'll be fine. Once you start playing, it's all the same."

But of course it wasn't the performance she was fretting

about. "What if he's not my father?" she said. "Or worse—what if he turns his back on me, as if I don't exist? Isn't that what he did when I was a child?"

"You don't know what happened back then."

She shrugged and choked back tears. "There aren't that many possibilities, are there?"

I embraced her. "I'll be there for you, Adriana, no matter what."

She nodded and picked up her viola case. "I'm all right now. Let's go."

We gave our names to the sentry at the gate. I had only known her as Adriana dalla Viola, so when she said, "Adriana Manzone," I squeezed her hand.

The Duke's retainers wore red doublets and green pants, the same colors as Modena's flag. Accompanied by a tall, bearded footman, one of these retainers led us up a grand staircase, down a wide corridor where portraits of previous Dukes hung on the walls, up a spiral staircase, and down two more corridors to what was clearly a music room, with a clavichord, a harp, and an assortment of other instruments. The two musicians who would complete our quartet awaited us in leather chairs. They were young men, cleanly shaved, wearing identical blue suits, the one tuning his cello, the other holding his violin.

They stood up, introduced themselves—Antonio and Maurizio were their names—and bowed. They knew who I was, but it was on Adriana that their gazes fell, and for good reason: the moment light touched her skin, whether sunlight or candlelight, her face grew even more radiant.

They had been informed of the program I had put together,

and they told me they had played the pieces several times. We had twenty minutes before the concert began. After tuning up together, we played the opening measures of the Scarlatti quartet that would be our first piece. I saw that Antonio and Maurizio were staring at my clarinet.

"I have never heard one before," Antonio remarked.

"In our final piece, the Albinoni," I said, "there are four solos, two for clarinet and two for violin. Adriana will play the string solos on the viola."

Adriana turned to me in surprise.

"I was prepared to play them," Antonio said, and I could see he was checking his temper.

"I understand that. And you will play the string solos in the other pieces."

"I am the first violinist in His Grace's orchestra," he added haughtily.

"Nevertheless, that is how we shall do it. Please don't take it as an affront."

Clearly he did, and Adriana was about to intercede when I said, "We don't have time to discuss it."

Maurizio had grown increasingly uneasy. "Antonio, His Grace ordered us to follow the lead of Signor Zen."

"Fine," Antonio said, sitting up very straight. "And we shall."

Another retainer entered the room and informed us that the Duke would soon arrive in the hall, and so we ought to take the stage now. Then he handed us each a two-page musical score. "The Duke begs your indulgence, Signor Zen, and asks that you play this capriccio at the conclusion of your program. As a special favor to him."

No name was printed on the score.

"Who is the composer?" I asked.

"That is a surprise, and I cannot say."

"Surprise for whom?"

"For the audience, signor. Now, please, follow me or we will arrive after His Grace, and that cannot be allowed to happen."

We followed him down yet another corridor, Adriana and I trailed by the two string players, to a set of double doors beneath the heraldic crest of Modena: a crowned eagle atop three blue fleurs-de-lys. The retainer opened the doors, and we walked onto a stage brightly lit beneath a crystal chandelier, and there before us an audience of about a hundred people who fell silent, following us with their eyes as we took our places. The hall had a high ceiling with a fresco of Saint Jerome on a mountaintop, and on the walls gigantic murals of other biblical scenes, from Ezekiel in his fiery chariot to the three Magi, surrounded by angels, beneath a starry sky. Gold draperies framed the windows. The floor was gleaming Carrara marble. The audience was what I had expected: gentlemen with extravagant wigs in velvet suits and ladies wearing silk gowns and a good deal of jewelry.

Onstage there were four chairs and music stands, backdropped by a red curtain. Adriana sat between Antonio and Maurizio, and I stood to their right. We did a second tuning, and opened our sheet music. I was most curious about the capriccio, and as I scanned the score, I realized who the composer must be even before everyone stood up and the Duke of Modena entered the hall with his surprise guest.

It was the Master himself, Antonio Vivaldi, acknowledging the applause of the audience and walking three paces behind the Duke.

I heard Adriana gasp, and I was so stunned that, after bowing formally to the Duke, I had to make an effort not to avert my eyes from him and Vivaldi in the front row. I glanced at Adriana: I knew it was difficult enough for her to look upon the Duke for the first time; to have the Master there, too, must have been overwhelming.

The Master hadn't changed much since I left the Ospedale: in a blue suit, with a bright yellow cravat, his long red hair half combed, half tangled, he seemed preoccupied. I guessed that he was in Modena seeking the Duke's patronage for one of his new operas. When he turned to the stage, I saw that he recognized Adriana at once and was puzzled to see her there. He looked at me with curiosity, for he had heard of the young clarinetist who was championing his compositions in European salons and concert halls. But as he studied my features, his curiosity obviously deepened, and despite my short hair and my fine clothes—for, after all, even then there were still only a handful of virtuoso clarinetists on the continent—he saw that I was Nicolà Vitale, who had disappeared from the Ospedale. His jaw dropped, he turned to the Duke to say something, then thought better of it, and folding his hands in his lap, wearing a bemused expression, he sat back to hear the music.

As for the Duke, at whom Adriana kept stealing glances, he wore a handsome white suit and green vest over a black silk shirt. He was a tall, thin man who looked younger than his years: his long, curly hair still black, with a spray of white above the ears, his eyes dark brown and penetrating, his face angular, with a long nose, thin lips, and a pointed chin. An intelligent face, sad but not angry, and behind the gaze of the absolute, unwavering ruler, a hint of kindness. I could not say the same for the woman beside him, obviously his sister, the Baronessa Casina, stout and sallow, her face locked in a grimace, her eyes narrowed, her lips shut tight. On her right was her daughter, equally sallow, but rail-thin, with a blank expression and washed-out eyes that roamed from object to object, never settling in any one place.

The Duke nodded for us to begin. I bowed to him again, and signaled the others to launch the Corelli sonata, and suddenly I was playing along with them and we were filling the hall with music. And with so many distractions—the Duke, Adriana, and now the Master, for whom I wanted to play that much better—I had to concentrate harder than ever. I had to remind myself yet again that, having performed so much great music with the help of my clarinet, under the most intense conditions, I really had trained my fingers and my ear, my heart and my mind, and yes, my soul, and had begun making myself into the musician I hoped to be. I felt a surge of joy, too, when I realized that, of all the factors animating my performance, one I couldn't have predicted—the love I shared with Adriana—had been the most crucial of all.

As we proceeded through the program, receiving strong applause after each piece, I didn't make eye contact with the Master. But I noticed that the Duke couldn't take his eyes off of Adriana. He seemed mesmerized, his expression certainly not lustful, or even admiring, but haunted. I had no idea what Adriana's mother had looked like, but I realized Adriana must bear a strong resemblance to her.

When we performed the final piece, the Albinoni, I completed my solo, and then turned the lead over to Adriana, who played a brilliant solo, with gusto, bringing the audience to its feet. I felt a tremendous rush of joy for her—and relief for me.

For our encore, we delivered a spirited rendition of the Master's capriccio. Considering we had never played it before, we did so with a surprising lack of errors. It was a delightful, intricate piece—much of it played *prestissimo*, which oddly forced us to work more from instinct—and as we concluded, the Duke led the applause, while the Master, not always the most gracious of men, bowed to us, studying me with a bemused smile.

Then the Duke beckoned Adriana and me over. "Thank you for visiting our court, Signor Zen. It was a fine performance."

"It was an honor, Your Excellency."

He turned to Adriana. "And you, my dear, played beautifully. Tell me, what is your name?"

Adriana curtsied. "Thank you, Your Excellency. My name is Adriana." She paused. "Adriana Manzone."

The Duke turned pale. But he didn't look surprised; if anything, it appeared as if his suspicions were being confirmed, but remained too fantastic for him to absorb. "A pretty name," he said. "Do you also hail from Venice?"

"Yes, but I was born here in Modena."

"I know most of my subjects. From what family are you?"

She lowered her eyes, then looked at him directly. "My mother was Heléne Manzone."

The Duke did not blink; but I could see that, as a man accustomed to keeping his feelings under wraps, he was having difficulty. The Baronessa, meanwhile, showed no sign of recognizing

 258

the name Heléne Manzone, but knew her brother well enough to sense his emotions. "What is it, Rinaldo?"

He ignored her, and said to Adriana, "So you grew up in Modena?"

"Only for the first four years of my life. Then my former nanny left me at the Ospedale della Pietà in Venice." She nodded toward the Master. "I was in the *privileggiate di coro*."

"The best of the best," Vivaldi put in.

"You are the girl who wrote the letters," the Baronessa exclaimed, covering her mouth.

"What letters?" the Duke said.

Adriana and I exchanged glances.

"She's an impostor!" the Baronessa cried, falling back into her chair.

"What are you saying?" the Duke snapped, but I knew from his voice that he had already intuited exactly what she was saying. He turned back to Adriana. "When did you leave Modena, my dear?"

"October 1705. From that time, until last month, I lived at the Ospedale. My mother died that same year, two months later. I never saw her again."

"My god," the Duke said under his breath.

The Baronessa had turned red, and the audience was buzzing now.

"I'm sorry," the Duke said. "I knew your mother. Do you remember where you lived with her?"

"I don't know the name of the street. It was a house with blue shutters and a blue roof. There were flowers on the porch." She paused. "My mother had a dog named Pépe. A white dog."

There were tears in the Duke's eyes. "Then you know who I am," he said softly.

She nodded.

"And that is why you came here this evening."

"Yes."

He looked at the Baronessa and said acidly, "I never received any letters. I'm sorry for that, Adriana, and for so much else." He opened his arms. "Come, child."

She stepped into his embrace.

The Baronessa was incredulous. "What are you saying?"

He held Adriana close. "What do you think I'm saying? This is my daughter. I am her father."

"Rinaldo!"

"All these years, I thought you were dead, Adriana," he said, choking back his sobs. "When she was gravely ill, your mother told me you had died. Before that, I would not formally adopt you, I would not even spend time with you, because I was so afraid of scandal. Heléne must have been even more afraid, and rightfully so, that when she died, you would be abandoned completely. So she took you away. And thinking you had died, I lived with my guilt for all these years. I ask you to forgive me."

"I do," Adriana said, tears welling up in her eyes. I knew that, though she had dreamed of an outcome like this when we traveled to Modena, she didn't really believe it could happen.

"Forgive you?" the Baronessa said scornfully. "Have you taken leave of your senses? This girl is a traveling musician. And who is Heléne Manzone—a woman you slept with?"

"Beatrice!" he said, with such menace that even the Baronessa's mute, impassive daughter, Maria Angela, recoiled.

"Anyone could tell you the things she has: a house with blue shutters, a white dog—"

"I am not going to warn you again," the Duke growled.

Noticing that I had instinctively moved closer to Adriana during this exchange, he took stock of me for the first time as someone who was not just a fellow musician. "How do you come to know Adriana, Signor Zen?"

Before I could reply, the Baronessa leaped up, fuming, and shouted, "I've had enough of this."

The Duke disengaged gently from Adriana. "And I've had enough of you, sister. I am telling you now, unequivocally and before witnesses, that this changes everything between us."

"You can't mean the succession?"

"*Everything.*" He raised his voice so everyone could hear. "It's a miracle, but I have a child again, my own issue."

"Not legitimate!" the Baronessa retorted.

"I say what is legitimate in Modena," he said with a clenched jaw. "Don't ever speak to me like that again, or you will not only be unwelcome here, but in Casina as well."

"You wouldn't dare."

"No? Father arranged for you to assume that title and all that went with it. I can take it away just as easily."

He turned to the astonished audience. "Friends, let me tell you what all the citizens of Modena will soon learn: this is my daughter, Adriana. She has come home, and so long as she desires it—and I hope that is well beyond my lifetime—this will be her home."

The Baronessa glared at him, then at Adriana and me, and grabbing Maria Angela's arm, stalked from the room.

The Duke put his arm around Adriana. "We have a lot of time to make up. We can only begin tonight. And, if you are willing, we shall visit the Archbishop tomorrow, so I can right things, as I should have years ago."

Listening inteltly to all of this, Vivaldi came up beside me and said, "You and I also have things to discuss, Nicolò. Perhaps later, over a glass of wine."

7

The Duke insisted on ordering up an impromptu supper for all his guests at the concert: roasted meats and fowl, aged cheeses and poached pears, figs and olives from the palace orchards, and the best and oldest red wine in the cellar. While he saw to the arrangements, Adriana and I had a few minutes alone in the music room.

"I'm scared, Nicolò. A part of me wants to run away."

"A man once told me that there are many things to fear in life, but despite what anyone tells you, good fortune is not one of them."

"He abandoned me once. . . ."

"He's naming you his heir. Declaring it before his Archbishop and his entire domain."

"I know. And you? You will continue your career, of course."

"I will."

"And return to Vienna?"

"No. Nor to Venice."

"Where, then?"

"That depends on your father, the Duke."

Her face lit up. "You mean—"

"But he may have other ideas. There are a good many Princes and Dukes who may come knocking at his door."

"They can knock all they like," she said defiantly. "If he turns you away, he is turning me away." She embraced me. "And I'm going to tell him that right now."

"Adriana, there's already been a lot of excitement tonight. Why not give it a day or two, and we can go to him together and do it properly."

"You're right. I just want him to know how happy we are."

"He will see that for himself. What he needs to know is that you want him to be happy, too."

"Oh, I do." She kissed me and I held her close. "But only if he says yes."

 264

IX
Coda

1

Six months later, Adriana and I were married. The Archbishop performed the ceremony in the cathedral. Master Vivaldi himself conducted the choir and afterward played a violin solo. The Duke invited all manner of people, including the Duke of Parma and the Crown Prince of Sardinia, the Count of Messina, the papal ambassador, and the general staff of his army. I had my own small guest list, all the Venetians who had helped me immeasurably when I was a poor boy in desperate straits: Bartolomeo Cattaglia and his sister, Signora Botello; Signora Gramani, the dressmaker; and Signora Capelli, still a resident of Mazzorbo, who saved my life and nursed me back to health after my family succumbed to malaria. Bartolomeo wore his old naval uniform, with all the medals he had been awarded for bravery, and Signora Capelli nearly fainted when she found herself seated behind the papal ambassador. Emmerich Hoyer traveled all the way from Vienna. And Adriana and I also invited Massimo Magnifico, but, to our disappointment, received word that he was on tour, currently in Rome, and would be unable to attend the wedding.

The Duke declared a week of celebration, and there were banquets and parties, dances and concerts, at the court and around the city. Adriana and I attended a great many of these, but none was so memorable as the last, which the Duke told us was a special surprise. It was at Modena's opera house, whose recent renovation the Duke had personally overseen. It was a full house, and there was a great deal of anticipation. Adriana and I were seated in the royal box with the Duke. We were expecting another concert, or perhaps one of the Master's latest operas, so we truly were surprised when Massimo Magnifico, resplendent in a red cape and gold turban, came out from behind the curtain with his primary assistant, our old friend Julietta. With a great flourish, and a broad smile, he bowed to our box, and proceeded to put on a show such as Modena had never seen before, according to the Duke.

It began with Julietta, attached to invisible wires, and beating long white wings, gliding to the ceiling of the opera house, where a dozen doves flew out from the folds of the wings. Julietta appeared as cool and calm as Meta once had, and assisted Massimo in nearly every feat he performed: transposing the members of the audience in the first and last rows; filling the pockets of all the men sitting on the aisles with copper coins; hurling six unlit candles into the air in quick succession, which Julietta, standing at the front of the stage, caught—burning now—and twirled until they exploded softly into silk banners. For a finale, Massimo stepped into one of the Chinese booths I had first seen at his villa and reappeared moments later at the back of our box, with a bouquet of orange roses for Adriana.

Many things have happened in the years since our wedding. I continued to perform in foreign cities, always traveling with Adriana, taking the opportunity to explore Paris and Madrid, Prague and Budapest, and venturing as far north as Saint Petersburg and as far south as Palermo. I accumulated a fortune of my own, and inspired the use of the clarinet in many far-flung ensembles, but after a while tired of the long trips and demanding performing schedules, and spent nearly all my time in Modena.

Enjoying access to the Duke's vast library, I read all the books of history, philosophy, and literature I could lay my hands on—Herodotus and Livy, Plutarch and Lucretius, Giovanni Boccaccio and Dante Alighieri, and of course Virgil, from whose epic the Duke could recite vast passages. I learned Latin and perfected my French and German. And it was because of this eclectic, but expansive, education that I acquired the skills and knowledge that enabled me to write the book you hold in your hands.

On our first anniversary, the Duke conferred upon me the title Prince of Mirandola, Modena's principality to the north, which included extensive landholdings and a spacious villa with a large garden that Adriana preferred to the palace in Modena. It was in Mirandola that she and I founded an orphanage for boys and girls, overseen by Bartolomeo and Signora Gramani. I used my influence, and Adriana her patronage, to bring a staff of fine musicians from every corner of Venetia to join us in teaching the children all the musical instruments necessary to form a small orchestra. Eventually this orchestra matched in quality, and rivaled in reputation, the *privileggiate di coro* at the Ospedale della Pietà.

I had no trouble getting used to being the husband of a Duchess, for I loved Adriana the same way after our marriage as I had before our arrival in Modena. But it did take time to accustom myself to being addressed as *Principe* by everyone I encountered, from people in the street to the Duke's royal acquaintances, but I expressly forbade Bartolomeo to ever call me that.

Massimo Magnifico, however, insisted on addressing me as

Principe. As you might expect, he took a sly, somewhat wicked, delight in doing so. Every summer he visited us and put on an outdoor show for the children of the orphanage, who had never encountered anyone like him before. He brought with him a menagerie of monkeys trained to juggle, a dancing fox, a dog that sang in the key of G, and a flock of mechanical birds that flew in circles over his head.

During one such visit, after he had entertained the children and they in turn had played him several pieces of music, he and Julietta dined with us in our villa. By this time, Julietta was not just Massimo's assistant, but his wife, having married him in a seaside ceremony on the island of Rhodes. Joining their retinue this time was an old crow that perched on Massimo's shoulder throughout the performance and at dinner sat on the windowsill watching us and waiting patiently for Massimo to retire for the night. I asked Massimo if the crow's name happened to be Téodor, and smiling, he gestured unconvincingly and said no, he had given him the name Carlo after he flew through his window one snowy night in Salzburg and remained with him ever since.

Massimo and Julietta were not only performing in Europe now, but had recently traveled to Istanbul and Baghdad, and then taken their tour clear across Asia, on the Silk Road, as far as Siam. They had many tales to tell. Especially riveting were the ones about the various wizards, sorcerers, and necromancers they encountered in the East, many of whom shared the secrets of their trade with Massimo and even performed alongside him. Enticed by the prospect of learning spectacular feats unknown to other European magicians, Massimo and Julietta had often followed these men into the remotest corners of these distant countries:

 270

mountain hideaways in Circassia, desert caves in Egypt, and a bamboo fortress built upon stilts in a jungle river in India.

The most amazing of all, according to Massimo, sipping from a goblet of black wine, was an underground compound outside Baghdad, where all the buildings were glass, and the sole inhabitant, a one-hundred-year-old shaman who looked not a day over thirty, played a flute very much like my clarinet that made all the glass vibrate in harmony with his music. Massimo and Julietta planned to return there the following spring, and they invited Adriana and me to accompany them. We were sorely tempted to see and hear such wonders.

But that is a story for another day. . . .

ACKNOWLEDGMENTS

I would like to thank my editor, Nancy Hinkel, for her encouragement and dedication, and my agent, Anne Sibbald, for all her support over the years.

ABOUT THE AUTHOR

Nicholas Christopher is the author of six novels: *The Soloist*, *Veronica*, *A Trip to the Stars*, *Franklin Flyer*, *The Bestiary*, and *Tiger Rag*; eight volumes of poetry, including *Crossing the Equator: New & Selected Poems*; and a nonfiction book, *Somewhere in the Night: Film Noir & the American City*. Over the years, he has been a regular contributor to the *New Yorker*, *Granta*, the *Paris Review*, and other magazines. His work has been widely translated and published in other countries, and he has received numerous awards and fellowships, from the Guggenheim Foundation, the Academy of American Poets, the Poetry Society of America, and the National Endowment for the Arts, among other institutions. A professor in the School of the Arts at Columbia University, he lives in New York City.